THE LITTLE MERMAID and Other Fairy Tales

THE LITTLE MERMAID
and Other Fairy Tales

HANS CHRISTIAN ANDERSEN

New English versions with an
introduction by Neil Philip

Illustrated by Isabelle Brent

LITTLE, BROWN AND COMPANY
BOSTON NEW YORK TORONTO LONDON

A LITTLE, BROWN BOOK
First published in Great Britain in 1998
by Little, Brown and Company (UK)

Conceived, designed and produced by
The Albion Press Limited
Spring Hill, Idbury, Oxfordshire OX7 6RU

ISBN: 0-316-64431-5

A CIP catalogue for this book is available from the British Library.

Designer: Emma Bradford

Neil Philip would like to thank Niels and Carol Jensen
and Anne Eskild-Jensen for help and hospitality.

1 3 5 7 9 10 8 6 4 2

Colour origination by York House Graphics, London
Typesetting by York House Typograhhic, London
Printed in Hong Kong/China by South China Printing Co.

For Ann-Jeanette Campbell

N. P.

For Paul Anthony Cooper

I. B.

CONTENTS

INTRODUCTION

ON Sunday, September 18, 1825, the young Hans Christian Andersen—still a struggling and rather immature schoolboy at the age of twenty—confided to his diary: "I must carry out my work! I must paint for mankind the vision that stands before my soul in all its vividness and diversity; my soul knows that it can and will do this."

Though he was from a poor family and knew no one, this earnest young man had been taken up by some of Denmark's most influential people; the king himself approved a grant from a royal fund to provide his belated education, and future grants were to support the struggling writer.

Andersen's curious combination of hypersensitivity and unshakeable self-belief—nakedly displayed in *The Diaries of Hans Christian Andersen* (1990)—carried him through numerous false starts until he found the medium in which he could paint his vision for mankind: the fairy tale. In Andersen's hands this art form—the storytelling vehicle of the dreams and longings of the unlettered—became a subtle method of autobiography. Andersen himself takes the central role in nearly all his tales, whether disguised as a student, a gardener, a mermaid, or a shirt collar; when he came to publish an actual autobiography, he entitled it *The Fairy Tale of My Life*.

In that book, Andersen recalls how as a child he often used to visit the spinning-room of the pauper hospital and asylum in Odense, Denmark, where he was brought up. The old women there, entertained by Andersen's childish prattle, rewarded him "by telling me tales in return; and thus a world as rich as that of *The Thousand and One Nights* was revealed to me." That rich world of the Danish folk tale—later harvested by collectors such as Evald Tang Kristensen, and analyzed by folklorist Bengt Holbek in his book *The Interpretation of Fairy Tales* (1987)—formed the soil in which Andersen's creativity could flower.

In 1857, Andersen stayed with Charles Dickens in England for five weeks. Although the two men had great respect for each other, the visit was a strain—Dickens's daughter Kate cruelly but succinctly summed up the family's view when she recalled, "He was a bony bore, and stayed on and on." Dickens himself—scrupulously polite and attentive to his guest—relieved his feelings afterward by sticking a notice on the dressing-room mirror which read, "Hans Andersen slept in this room for five weeks—which seemed to the family AGES!"

The main problem was that Andersen's spoken English was almost incomprehensible. Andersen's first translator, Mary Howitt, spitefully assured Dickens that in fact Andersen didn't know Danish either. There is an edge to this comment. Andersen's Danish is not the severe, highflown literary Danish of his day—it is raw and unpolished, and in it one is always aware of the speaking voice. This directness and informality, both of phrasing and rhythm, stem directly from the storytelling of the old women in the Odense spinning-room, and they are one of the reasons why Andersen's fairy tales have stayed so fresh and appealing.

This colloquial quality was not always apparent in Victorian translations such as Mary Howitt's, which gave Andersen's tales a genteel and overworked air; one of my aims in making these new versions of some of Andersen's finest tales is to follow modern translators such as R. P. Keigwin and Brian Alderson in capturing his relaxed and intimate storytelling voice.

Interestingly, Andersen *did* connect with the Dickens children, when he was able to tell them stories, not with his voice, but with his scissors. Henry Dickens recalled, "He had one beautiful accomplishment, which was the cutting out in paper, with an ordinary pair of scissors, of lovely little figures of sprites and elves, gnomes, fairies, and animals of all kinds, which might well have stepped out of the pages of his books. These figures turned out to be quite delightful in their refinement and delicacy in design and touch."

Many of Andersen's paper cuttings survive: they can be seen at the H. C. Andersen Museum in Odense, or enjoyed in books such as Beth Wagner Brust's *The Amazing Paper Cuttings of Hans Christian Andersen* (1994). In "Little Ida's Flowers," Andersen portrays himself as the student who entertains Ida with both stories and paper cuttings; the cuttings themselves play a key role in "The Steadfast Tin Soldier."

Stories such as "Little Ida's Flowers" and "The Little Match Girl," which have always been among his most popular, have led some modern writers—for instance John Goldthwaite in *The Natural History of Make-Believe* (1996)—to criticize Andersen for his "sentimentality." Yet this "sentimentality" of Andersen's is a strange thing. At the heart of his vision of the world lies the ability to find comedy in tragedy. Story after story ends sadly in rejection, humiliation, or disappointment, yet they are saved from self-pity by the "salt" of Andersen's wit and by the acuteness of his observation.

That Andersen is essentially a poet of human suffering can be seen in one of his finest and most famous stories, "The Little Mermaid." Andersen felt driven to write this original fairy tale, of which he wrote that while "only an adult can understand its deeper meaning" nevertheless "I believe a child will enjoy it for the story's sake." The story is now perhaps best known in Disney's more optimistic version—but the deeper meaning resides in Andersen's bleak and painful original.

"The Little Mermaid" was the first fairy tale in which Andersen attempted to explore his spiritual beliefs. A later story, "The Bell," expresses his deep faith in the beauty and holiness of the world, and the promise of new life and redemption beyond it. In it, two boys, one

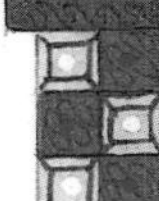

"a king's son," the other a pauper, make their way by separate routes—one in sunshine, the other in shadow—to the same transcendent moment at the end of their (life's) journey.

Both of the boys in this strange and moving tale are depictions of Andersen himself—they reassure him, and us, that a humble beginning and a difficult path will not make any difference in the end. The story, published in 1842, looks back to 1819, Andersen's confirmation year—the year in which he met and played with a real king's son, Prince Frederik, the future King Frederik VII of Denmark. In later life Andersen and Frederik were on close terms; Elias Bredsdorff records in *Hans Christian Andersen: The Story of His Life and Work* (1975) that the king treated the storyteller "almost like an old friend."

In 1987, the Danish historian Jens Jørgensen published an extraordinary and controversial book entitled *H. C. Andersen: En Sand Myte* (*H. C. Andersen: A True Myth*), in which he constructed an intricate web of circumstantial evidence to support his theory that Andersen was in fact the illegitimate son of King Christian VIII (Prince Frederik's father) and Countess Elise Ahlefeldt-Laurvig.

Jørgensen makes a good case both that such a child existed, and that Andersen himself was quite possibly "adopted" by his impoverished parents. He also establishes a pattern of royal and aristocratic patronage of the gawky pauper boy which suggests that someone important was keeping a weather eye out for the lad.

Though he does not firmly establish his theory as fact, Jørgensen does show that Andersen himself probably came to believe it. In a diary entry for January 3, 1875, the last year of his life, Andersen remarks how many letters he has received, then adds drily, "One has my name and address: King Christian the Ninth."

This intriguing theory, which caused a sensation in Denmark, has been rejected by some scholars, such as Elias Bredsdorff. But while it must be treated with caution, it does provide a fascinating new context in which to view the "fairy tale" of Andersen's life, and in which to read

a story such as "The Bell." Is it of significance that the boy is always described as "a king's son," never as "a prince"? Was Andersen imagining how much easier his life's path might have been, if his childish boastings that he was really "a changed child of noble birth" were true? If so, his conclusion is that the path in sunshine and the path in shadow lead to the same final destination.

It was about "The Bell" that Andersen made his famous comment that his fairy tales "lay in my mind like seed-corn, requiring only a mountain stream, a ray of sunshine, a drop of wormwood, for them to spring forth and burst into bloom."

Nearly two hundred years after his birth, his garden of fairy tales is still in full flower.

NEIL PHILIP

THE TINDERBOX

L*EFT, right! Left, right!*

A soldier came marching down the road. He had a pack on his back and a sword at his side. He was coming home from the wars.

On the way he met an old witch. She was so ugly, her lower lip hung right down to her chest. "Good evening, handsome," she said. "I can see from your pack and your sword that you are a real soldier. How would you like to be rich?"

"I'd like it very much, old witch," said the soldier.

"Do you see that big tree over there?" said the witch, pointing to a tree nearby. "It's quite hollow inside. If you climb to the top, you can get in and lower yourself to the bottom. I'll tie a rope around your waist so I can pull you back up when you call."

"Why should I do that?" asked the soldier.

"To fetch the treasure!" said the witch. "Now, listen. When you get to the bottom you will find yourself in a wide passage lit by over a hundred lamps. You will see three doors, with keys in the locks. If you go through the first door you will see a large chest, guarded by a dog with eyes as big as saucers. But don't worry about him! I'll lend you my blue-and-white checked apron. Just spread it on the floor, and lift the dog down off the chest and onto the apron. Then you can open the chest and take out as many coins as you like. But they're only coppers. If you want silver, you'll have to go through the second door.

"Behind that is a dog with eyes as big as soup plates. But don't mind him! Just put him on the apron, and take the money.

"Or if you'd prefer gold, go through the third door. The dog in there is a bit of a caution—eyes as big as cartwheels! But don't worry. Just put him on the apron and he won't hurt you. Then you can take as much gold as you can carry."

"That's all very well," said the soldier, "but what do you get out of it, witch? I've no doubt you'll want your cut."

"No," said the witch, "I won't take a single penny. All I want is an old tinderbox, for its sentimental value. My granny left it behind by mistake last time she was down there."

"Let's get on with it then," said the soldier. "Tie the rope around my waist."

"There you are," said the witch, "and here is the apron."

So the soldier climbed the tree and lowered himself down the hole in the trunk, until he came to the wide passage lit by over a hundred lamps, just as the witch had promised.

He opened the first door. Oh! There was the dog with eyes as big as saucers, glaring at him.

"Good dog!" he said. He set it down on the witch's apron, opened the chest, and took as many copper coins as he could cram into his pockets. Then he shut the chest and lifted the dog back onto it.

He opened the second door. Ah! There was the dog with eyes as big as soup plates. "Don't stare at me like that!" said the soldier. "You'll strain your eyes." And he set the dog down on the apron. When he saw all the silver coins in the chest, he threw away the copper ones and filled his pockets and his pack with silver.

He opened the third door. Ugh! There was the dog with eyes as big as cartwheels—and they were spinning round in his head!

"Good evening," said the soldier, and he saluted, for he had never seen such a dog in his life. For a while the soldier just stood there looking at him, but then he said to himself, *Enough of this!* and lifted the dog down onto the apron.

When he opened the chest—my goodness what a lot of gold there

was! Enough to buy up the whole city of Copenhagen, and all the gingerbread men and tin soldiers and rocking horses in the world. There was an absolute fortune.

So the soldier cast aside the silver coins and filled his pockets and his pack with gold instead; he even stuffed it down his boots and in his cap. He could hardly move—but he was rich!

He put the dog back on the chest, slammed the door behind him, and called up through the hollow tree, "Pull me up, you old witch!"

"Have you got the tinderbox?" asked the witch.

"No," said the soldier, "I'd clean forgotten it." He went back to fetch it, and then the witch hauled him up. Then he was standing back on the road, with his pockets and his pack, his boots and his cap filled with gold.

"What's so special about the tinderbox?" he asked.

"Mind your own business," snapped the witch. "You've got your money. Just give me the box."

"Stuff and nonsense!" said the soldier. "Tell me what it's for or I'll cut off your head."

"No!" said the witch.

So he cut off her head. There she lay!

The soldier bundled up all his gold in her apron and slung it over his shoulder, tucked the tinderbox in his pocket, and set off to town.

It was fine town, and the soldier checked into the finest hotel in the place. He stayed in the best rooms and ordered the choicest things on the menu, because now he was a rich man with money to burn.

The servant who cleaned his boots did think it was odd that such a wealthy man should have such shabby shoes—for the soldier hadn't had time to buy anything yet. But next day the soldier kitted himself out with smart clothes and new boots, and then he really looked the part of a fashionable gentleman. Everyone wanted to know him. They boasted to him about their town, and about their king and his beautiful daughter.

"I'd like to see her," said the soldier.

"No one can see her," they answered. "She lives in a copper castle surrounded by walls and towers. The king doesn't let anyone in to see her, because it was foretold that she will marry a common soldier, and the king doesn't like that idea at all."

Wouldn't I like to get a look at her! thought the soldier, but it was no use thinking of that.

His life now was a merry one. And when he went to the theatre, or out riding in his carriage, he gave away lots of money to the poor, because he remembered when his own pockets had been empty.

Now that he was rich and well dressed, he had many friends. They all told him how generous he was, and that this was the mark of a true gentleman, and the soldier liked that. But as he was spending money like water and never earning any more, he was soon down to his last two coppers. He had to leave his fine suite and move to a poky little room in the attic. Now he had to polish his own boots and darn his own clothes. None of his new friends ever came to see him; they said there were too many stairs to climb.

One evening he was sitting in the dark, without even a candle, when he remembered that he had seen a candle stub in the tinderbox when he fetched it out of the tree for the old witch. So he got out the candle stub, and struck a spark from the tinderbox.

As soon as he had done so, the door sprang open, and there was the dog with eyes as big as saucers, saying, "What is your command, master?"

What's going on here? thought the soldier. *This is a funny sort of tinderbox. Can I have whatever I want?* And he said to the dog, "Bring me some money!" It was gone and back in a flash, and when it returned it was carrying a big sack of copper coins in its mouth.

Now the soldier began to appreciate what a special tinderbox it was. If he struck it once it summoned the dog who guarded the copper coins; twice, the dog who guarded the silver; three times, the dog who guarded the gold.

So the soldier was able to move back into his old rooms and buy more fine clothes, and all his friends remembered him and took up with him just where they had left off.

One night he was sitting by himself and thinking about the princess. *It's a shame that no one can see her. It doesn't matter how lovely she is if she's kept hidden away in that copper castle. If only I could see her!* And then he thought, *Where's that tinderbox?*

He struck a spark, and the dog with eyes as big as saucers came. "I know it's the middle of the night," the soldier said, "but all the same I'd like to see the princess, if only for a minute."

Away went the dog, and before the soldier could think things over he had returned with the sleeping princess lying on his back. Anyone could see she was a true princess, she was so beautiful. The soldier kissed her. He couldn't help himself—he was a real soldier.

The dog ran straight back to the copper castle with the princess. At breakfast next morning she told her father and mother about the strange dream she had had. "I was riding on a dog's back, and a soldier kissed me."

The queen pursed her lips. "A nice kind of dream that is!" she said. And she insisted that one of her ladies-in-waiting must watch over the princess that night, just in case.

The soldier longed to see the princess again, and so that night he sent the dog to fetch her. And although the dog was very fast, the old lady who was watching over the princess had just time to pull on her boots and run after it. She saw the dog go into a big house. *Aha!* she thought. She chalked a white cross on the door, so that she would be able to find it in the morning. Then she went home to bed.

When the dog carried the princess back to the castle, he noticed the white cross on the soldier's door. So the dog took some chalk and put a cross on every door in town. It was a clever thing to do, because now the lady-in-waiting would never find the right door.

The next morning the king and the queen, the old lady-in-waiting, and all the court went out to see where the princess had been.

"Here it is!" exclaimed the king, when he saw a door with a cross in it.

"No, it's here, dear," said the queen, who had seen another door with a cross.

"Here's one!"

"Here's another!"

Wherever they looked, every door had a cross. So they gave up.

But the queen had quick wits; she was good for more than just riding around in a carriage. She took her gold scissors and cut out some silk and sewed it into a pretty bag, which she filled with fine white flour. That evening, she tied the bag to the princess's waist and then made a tiny hole in it with her scissors, so that if the princess moved, flour would leak out.

That night the dog came once more to fetch the princess. The soldier loved her so. How he wished he were a prince so that he could marry her.

The dog never noticed the flour, which made a trail all the way from the castle to the soldier's room. So in the morning the king and queen could see where their daughter had been taken. They had the soldier arrested and thrown into prison.

And there he sat in the dark, with nothing to do but listen to them saying, "You'll be hanged tomorrow!" It wasn't much fun. And what's worse, the tinderbox had been left behind at the hotel.

In the morning, the soldier looked through the iron bars of his cell and watched the people going out of town to the place where the gallows had been set up. The royal guards marched past to the sound of drums. Everyone was in a hurry to see him hanged.

Last of all was a shoemaker's apprentice, in his leather apron and slippers. As he cantered along, one of his slippers fell off and landed right outside the soldier's window.

"Hey!" shouted the soldier. "Apprentice! Not so fast! They can't start without me. If you will go to my room and fetch me my tinderbox, and be quick about it, I'll give you four coppers."

The shoemaker's apprentice was very glad of the chance to earn four coppers, so he sprinted off at the double to fetch the tinderbox and bring it back to the soldier.

And now you shall hear what happened then.

The gallows had been set up outside the town gates, and all the guards and the people were standing around it. The king and the queen were sitting on their thrones opposite the judge and the whole council.

The soldier had climbed the ladder, and the executioner was just about to fasten the noose around his neck. Then the soldier spoke up. He said it was the custom to grant a condemned man's last request; all he wanted was to smoke one last pipe of tobacco.

The king couldn't say no to that. So the soldier took his tinderbox and struck it—once, twice, three times! And there stood all three dogs: the one with eyes as big as saucers, the one with eyes as big as soup plates, and the one with eyes as big as cartwheels.

"Help me now. I don't want to be hanged!" shouted the soldier.

And the dogs fell on the judge and the councillors, tossing them high into the air—so high that when they fell back to the ground, they broke into pieces.

"Not me!" shrieked the king, but the biggest dog picked up both the king and the queen and flung them up into the air like the others.

The royal guards were frightened out of their wits, and the people shouted, "Little soldier, you shall be our king, and marry the princess!"

The soldier sat in the king's carriage, and the three dogs danced in front of it and barked, "Hurrah!" The guards presented arms, while little boys whistled through their fingers.

So the princess left her copper castle and became queen, which she liked much better. The wedding feast lasted for a week, and the dogs sat at the table, staring about them with their great glaring eyes.

LITTLE IDA'S FLOWERS

"MY poor flowers are nearly dead!" said little Ida. "Only last night they were so beautiful, and now they are withering." She showed them to the student who was sitting on the sofa. She was very fond of him, because he used to tell her wonderful stories and could cut amazing pictures out of a piece of paper—hearts with little dancers in them, flowers, and great castles with doors that opened. He was a lighthearted young man.

"Why are they drooping so?" she asked.

"Don't you know?" replied the student. "They've been dancing all night. They are exhausted; that is why they are hanging their heads."

"But flowers can't dance," said Ida.

"Oh yes they can," said the student. "After dark, when we are all tucked up in our beds, the flowers hop around quite gaily. They hold a ball nearly every night."

"Can their children go to the ball too?" asked Ida.

"Yes, both the daisies and the lilies-of-the-valley can go."

"And where do the loveliest flowers dance?"

"Do you remember the flower garden of the king's summer palace, where you go to feed bread to the swans? That's where the grand ball is held."

"I went there yesterday with Mother," said Ida. "But there wasn't a leaf on the trees, and there were no flowers at all. Where can they have gone? There are so many in the summertime."

"The king and queen move to the city for the winter, and as soon as they have gone, the flowers move into the palace and have a wonderful time. You should see them! The two loveliest roses go and sit on the throne and act the king and queen. The red cockscombs line up along both sides and bow, like gentlemen of the court. Then all the most beautiful flowers come in, and the grand ball begins. The blue violets are young naval cadets, and they dance with the hyacinths and crocuses, whom they call Miss. The tulips and the big yellow lilies are like old dowagers, and they keep an eye on things and make sure there's no hanky-panky."

"But," interrupted Ida, "surely the flowers aren't allowed to hold a ball in the king's palace."

"Nobody knows anything about it," said the student. "Once in a while the old night watchman who looks after the castle walks through it, but he carries a great bunch of keys, and when they hear the keys rattling, all the flowers hide. Sometimes the night watchman sniffs the air, and thinks to himself, *I'm sure I can smell flowers*, but he has never seen them."

"Oh, what fun!" said little Ida, and she clapped her hands. "But could I see the flowers?"

"Of course," said the student. "Next time you are there, just peep through the windows, and you'll be sure to see them. Only today I saw a long yellow daffodil reclining on a sofa, pretending to be a lady-in-waiting."

"What about the flowers in the botanical garden—could they go to the ball? It's a long way."

"Yes, they could. If flowers really want to, they can fly. That's what butterflies are—flowers that jumped off their stems, flapped their petals, and flew away. Some of them never go back to their stems but grow real wings and flutter about all day. You must have often seen it.

"It may be that the flowers in the botanical garden have never heard what goes on in the palace. Next time you are there, lean over and whisper to one of the flowers, 'There's a grand ball at the summer palace tonight,' and then just wait and see. Flowers can't keep a secret; they'll whisper it from one to another, and at nightfall they'll all fly away. The professor who looks after them will go into the garden and find all the flowers gone. That will give him something to think about!"

"But how can the flowers tell each other about the ball? They can't speak."

"Not in words," said the student. "They communicate by mime. You must have seen them nodding and swaying in the breeze. They can understand each other just as well as we can by talking."

"Does the professor understand them?" asked Ida.

"He most certainly does! Why, one morning he went into the garden and saw a hulking great stinging nettle rustling its leaves at a pretty little red carnation. It was saying, *I love you, dreamboat*. Now the professor doesn't like that kind of talk, so he rapped the nettle over its fingers—its leaves, you would call them. But the nettle stung him, and ever since the professor has been afraid to touch a nettle."

Ida laughed. "What fun!"

But the grumpy old councillor who was also sitting in the room said, "Fancy filling a child's head with such rubbish!" He didn't like the student one bit. When the student made one of his funny papercuts—it might be of a man hanging from a gallows with a heart in his hand, who had been condemned for stealing hearts, or an old witch riding on a broomstick, with her husband balanced on her nose—the councillor would always mutter, "Such rubbish to put into a child's head! What tomfoolery!"

But Ida thought what the student had said was very funny, and she kept on thinking about it. She was sure that the flowers were hanging their heads because they were tired out from dancing all night. She took them over to the little table where her playthings were, and where her doll Sophie was sleeping in her cradle. Ida said, "You must be a good doll, Sophie, and let the flowers sleep in your bed tonight, for they are ill and need to be made better. You can sleep in the drawer." Sophie never said a word, but she looked cross at having to give up her bed to the flowers.

Ida laid the faded flowers in her doll's bed, tucked them in, and told them to lie quiet while she made them a cup of tea. "You'll feel much better in the morning," she said. Then she drew the curtains around the bed so that the sun wouldn't shine in their eyes.

All that evening she kept thinking about what the student had told her. At bedtime, she went to the window and peeped behind the curtains at her mother's tulips and hyacinths in their pots, and whispered, "I know where you are going tonight." The flowers acted as though they hadn't understood; they never stirred a leaf. But Ida knew what was what.

Once she was in bed, Ida lay awake thinking how lovely it would be to see the beautiful flowers dancing in the king's palace. *I wonder if my flowers have really been there?* she thought, and then she was asleep.

In the middle of the night, she woke; she had been dreaming about the flowers, and how the councillor had scolded the student for filling her head with rubbish. It was very quiet in her bedroom; the night-light was burning on the table beside her; her mother and father were asleep.

I wonder if my flowers are still lying in Sophie's bed, she thought. *I would love to know!* She sat up in bed and looked through the open door to the room in which the flowers were. She thought she could hear a piano playing, soft and sweet.

Now all the flowers are dancing. Oh! If only I could see them! But she didn't dare get up, for fear of waking her mother and father.

If only they would come in here! she thought. But the flowers never came, though the beautiful music kept playing. She couldn't bear it any longer. She crept out of bed, tiptoed to the door, and looked into the next room.

There was no night-light, but it wasn't dark, because the moon was shining through the window onto the floor. It was nearly as bright as day. All the tulips and hyacinths were standing in two long rows on the floor; they had left their flowerpots behind on the windowsill. The flowers danced so prettily on the floor, holding on to each other's leaves and swinging each other around.

A tall yellow lily was playing the piano. Ida remembered seeing it in the garden that summer, because the student had said, "It looks just like Miss Lena!" And although everyone had laughed at him then, Ida now thought that the flower did look just like Miss Lena; it had the same trick of turning its face from side to side as it played, and nodding in time to the music.

None of the flowers noticed little Ida.

Now a tall blue crocus leaped right up onto the table and drew back the curtains from the cradle where the sick flowers were lying. They looked quite well again, and they wanted to join in. The old porcelain chimney sweep with the chipped chin stood up and bowed to them, and then they were swept off into the dance.

Something fell from the table with a crash. It was a bundle of sticks tied together with ribbons into a switch, which had been given to Ida for a carnival parade. It thought it was a flower too; and it did look fine, with its ribbons flying. It had three legs, and it could dance the mazurka, which none of the flowers could do because they couldn't stamp.

Now there was a little wax doll tied to the top of this switch, wearing a wide-brimmed hat just like the councillor's. All at once, this doll seemed to swell up, and it boomed, "Fancy filling a child's head with such nonsense! What tomfoolery!" It really did look just like the councillor, and Ida couldn't help laughing.

The switch kept dancing all this time, and whipping at the wax doll with its ribbons, so that the doll had to dance too, until the softhearted flowers begged it to stop.

Then came a knocking from the drawer. The little porcelain chimney sweep managed to open it a crack, and Sophie the doll poked her head out. "Is there a ball going on? Why wasn't I told?"

"May I have the pleasure of this dance?" asked the sweep.

"You? Dance with me?" said Sophie, and she sat down on the open drawer with her back to him. She thought that one of the flowers would ask her to dance; but none of them did. The chimney sweep had to dance on his own, and he didn't do badly at all.

Sophie coughed—*ahem! ahem!*—but still none of the flowers noticed her. So she let herself fall to the floor. She landed with a crash, and all the flowers ran up to her to ask whether she had hurt herself; Ida's flowers were especially concerned. But Sophie wasn't hurt in the slightest. Ida's flowers said thank you for the loan of the bed, and Sophie said they were quite welcome, and she was perfectly happy in the drawer. Then all the flowers danced around her in the middle of the floor, where there was a great splash of moonlight.

Sophie told the flowers they could keep her bed, but they replied, "Thank you, but we shan't need it. We don't live long; we shall be dead by the morning. Ask Ida to bury us in the garden, where the canary is buried. Next year we shall come to life again, and be even prettier."

"You mustn't die," said Sophie, and she kissed the flowers.

At that moment the door of the drawing room opened, and a troop of lovely flowers came dancing in. Ida could not think where they could have come from, if not from the king's palace. Two beautiful roses wearing crowns led the way. They were the king and queen. Behind them came the stocks and carnations, bowing to the company. There was even a band—poppies and peonies blowing on the pods of sweet peas until they were red in the face, and bluebells tinkling like real bells. It was a funny sort of orchestra.

At the end of the throng came all the dancing flowers—violets, daisies, and lilies-of-the-valley. It was lovely to see how they kissed each other at the end of the dance.

At last they said goodnight to one another, and little Ida crept back to bed, to dream of everything she had seen.

Next morning when she woke, she ran straight to the doll's cradle to see if the flowers were still there. They were, but they had withered and died. Sophie was still in the drawer; she looked very sleepy.

"Do you have something to tell me?" asked Ida; but Sophie just looked stupid and didn't say a word.

"You're very naughty," said Ida, "and yet all the flowers danced with you." Then she took a cardboard box with a picture of a bird on it and laid the flowers in it, saying, "When my cousins come from Norway, we shall bury you in the garden, so that you will come up again next year."

Ida's cousins were two lively boys called Jonas and Adolph. Their father had given them new bows and arrows, and they brought those with them to show Ida.

She told them all about the poor dead flowers, and the two boys came to the funeral. They walked in front, with their bows slung over their shoulders, and Ida followed with the dead flowers in their pretty coffin. They dug a hole in the corner of the garden. Then Ida kissed the flowers, and she laid them in the ground in their box. As they didn't have a gun or a cannon, Jonas and Adolph shot arrows over the grave.

THE LITTLE MERMAID

FAR out to sea the water is as blue as the petals of the loveliest cornflower and as clear as the purest glass; but it is deep, deeper than any anchor can reach. Countless church steeples would have to be piled one on top of the other to stretch from the sea bed to the surface. That's where the sea folk live.

Now you mustn't imagine that the bottom is just bare white sand; not at all. Wonderful trees and plants grow down there, with stems and leaves so sensitive that they curl and sway with the slightest movement of the water, as if they were living creatures. Fish, large and small, flit through the branches just like birds in the air up here.

At the very deepest point lies the palace of the sea king. Its walls are of coral, and the long, pointed windows are of the clearest amber. The roof is made of cockle shells that open and shut with the play of the waves. It's lovely to see, because nestling in each shell is a shining pearl, any one of which would be the pride of a queen's crown.

The sea king had been a widower for many years, but his old mother kept house for him. She was a wise old lady, but rather too proud of being royal; that's why she always wore twelve oysters on her tail, when the rest of the nobility were only allowed six. Aside from that she was a praiseworthy sort, and she took very good care of her granddaughters, the little sea princesses.

There were six of them, all beautiful, but the youngest was the loveliest of them all. Her skin was pure and clear as a rose petal, and her eyes were as blue as the deepest lake. But like all the others, she had no legs—her body ended in a fish's tail.

All the livelong day they would play down there in the palace, in its spacious apartments where living flowers grew from the walls. When the great amber windows were open, the fish would dart in and out, just as swallows do up here, and they would eat out of the princesses' hands and let themselves be petted.

Outside the castle was a great park with trees of deep blue and fiery red; their fruits shone like gold, and their flowers glowed like flames among the flickering leaves. The earth was of the finest sand, but blue as burning sulphur. Everything was suffused with blue, so that you might think you were high up in the air, with sky above and below you, rather than down at the bottom of the sea. When the sea was calm, you could glimpse the sun up above, like a crimson flower from which light came streaming down.

Each little princess had her own patch of garden, where she could plant whatever she fancied. One made a flowerbed in the shape of a whale; another preferred hers to look like a mermaid. But the youngest princess made hers round like the sun and would only plant flowers that shone red like it. She was a strange child, quiet and thoughtful. Her sisters' gardens were full of oddments salvaged from shipwrecks, but she had only the statue of a handsome boy in hers. It was carved from clear white marble, and it had sunk to the bottom of the sea when the ship that was carrying it was lost. Beside this statue she planted a rose-red weeping willow, which grew taller than it and shaded it with its overhanging branches. In the play of violet shadows on the blue sand, it looked as if the statue and the tree were embracing.

The princesses liked nothing more than to listen to stories of the world above. The old grandmother had to tell again and again everything she knew about ships, and towns, and people, and animals. The youngest princess was particularly taken with the idea that up above flowers were scented, for at the bottom of the sea they had no smell at all. She also liked to hear about the green forest, and how the fish that swam among the branches could sing so beautifully. Her

grandmother called birds "fish"—otherwise the princesses wouldn't have understood, for they had never seen a bird.

"When you turn fifteen," their grandmother would say, "you too will be able to swim to the surface and sit on rocks in the moonlight to watch the great ships sailing by. If you dare, you can swim close enough to the shore to see woods and towns."

The following year the oldest of the sisters would be fifteen. The others were each spaced about a year apart, so that the youngest would have to wait another five whole years before she was allowed to swim up from the sea bed and take a look at us. But each sister promised the others she would come back after her first day on the surface and tell all the exciting things she had seen. For their grandmother didn't tell them nearly enough—there was so much they wanted to know.

None of them was so full of yearning as the youngest—the one who had the longest time to wait, and who was so quiet and thoughtful. Many a night she stood at the open window and gazed up through the dark blue water. She could make out the moon and the stars, though they were pale and blurry beneath the sea. If a black cloud passed over, she knew it must be either a whale swimming overhead or else a ship sailing along the surface; the passengers and crew never dreaming that a lovely mermaid stood in the depths below them and stretched her white hands out to them.

Now the oldest sister was fifteen, and free to swim up to the surface. When she came back she had hundreds of things to tell. The loveliest thing of all, she said, was to lie in the moonlight on a sandbank when the sea was calm and look across to a seaport town, with its lights twinkling like stars, and music playing, and all the clatter of carts and people; she loved to watch and listen, and to see the church spires and hear the bells ringing. Though she knew she could never go there, yet her heart was filled with longing to.

The youngest princess hung on her every word. Late in the evening, as she stood dreaming at the open window and gazing up through the water, she thought so hard about the town that she imagined she could hear the church bells chime.

Next year the second sister got her freedom. She surfaced just as the sun was setting, and the sight was so ravishing she could barely describe it. The whole sky had been a blaze of gold, she said, and as for the clouds—she couldn't find words to capture their beauty as they sailed over her head, streaked with crimson and violet. A skein of wild swans had flown into the setting sun, as if drawing a white veil across the water. She had swum after them, but as the sun sank, so the vision of sea, sky, and cloud had faded.

The third of the sisters was the most daring of them all. She swam right inland up a broad river. She saw green hills covered with vines, castles, and farms hidden in the forest. She heard the birds singing, and the sun was so hot that she was often forced to dive back under water to cool her burning face. In a small cove she had come upon a group of human children splashing in the water, quite naked; but when she tried to play with them, they ran off in alarm. Then a little black animal—it was a dog, but she didn't know that—had come and barked at her so furiously that she took fright and headed out to sea. But she would never forget those magnificent woods and green hills, and those sweet little children who tried to swim in the water even though they had no tails.

The fourth sister was not so bold. She stayed well away from shore, and she said that there wasn't anything more beautiful than the open sea, with nothing for miles around and the sky above like a great glass bell. She had seen ships, but so far away they looked like seagulls. She had swum with the dolphins, who had turned somersaults for her, and the huge whales had sprayed jets of water into the air, like so many fountains.

The fifth sister's birthday fell in winter, so she saw something none of her sisters had seen. The sea looked quite green, and great icebergs were floating in it. They looked like pearls, yet each one was larger than a church tower. They had the strangest shapes, and they sparkled like diamonds. She had seated herself on one of the largest, and all the sailors had steered away in fear as they sailed past the iceberg where she sat with her long hair streaming in the wind. By evening a storm was blowing. The dark waves lifted the icebergs high up, and lightning flashed red on the ice. The ships had furled their sails and waited out the storm in terror, while she sat calmly on her iceberg and watched the blue lightning zigzag into the glittering sea.

The first time any of the sisters was allowed to go to the surface she was always delighted to see so many things that were new and beautiful. But when they were older and could go any time they liked, they soon lost interest; they wanted to be back home. The bottom of the ocean was the most beautiful place of all.

Still, many an evening the five sisters would link arms and rise to the surface together. They had lovely voices—more hauntingly beautiful than any human voice—and when a storm was blowing and they thought ships might be wrecked, they would swim in front of them and sing about all the wonders waiting at the bottom of the sea. Their song told the sailors not to be afraid of coming down—but the sailors could not make out the words in the howling storm. Nor did they ever see any of the delights of which the princesses sang, for when the ship sank the crew were drowned, and they came only as dead men to the palace of the sea king.

When the sisters floated up to the surface like this, arm in arm, their little sister stayed behind all alone. As she watched them go she would have cried, but a mermaid has no tears, and so she suffers all the more.

"If only I were fifteen!" she sighed. "I know that I shall love the world up there, and the people who live in it."

And then at last she was fifteen.

"There now! We're getting you off our hands at last," said her old grandmother. "Let me dress you up like your sisters." She set a garland of white lilies in her hair; each petal was half a pearl. Then she made eight big oysters pinch fast onto her tail, to show that she was a princess.

"Ow! That hurts," said the little mermaid.

"One must suffer to be beautiful," said her grandmother.

The little mermaid would have gladly swapped her heavy garland of pearls for some of the red flowers from her garden, which suited her much better, but she didn't dare.

"Goodbye," she said, and she floated up through the water as lightly as a bubble.

The sun had just set when she lifted her head above the water. The clouds still gleamed rose and gold, and in the pale pink sky the evening star shone clear and bright. The air was soft and fresh, and the sea was perfectly calm. A large three-masted ship lay close by. Only one sail was set, because there wasn't a breath of wind. The sailors were sitting idly in the rigging; below on the deck there was music and singing, and as the evening grew dark, hundreds of lanterns were lit, like so many flags.

The little mermaid swam to a porthole and the waves lifted her up so that she could see the smartly dressed people inside. The handsomest of all was a young prince with jet-black eyes. This was his sixteenth birthday, and that was the cause of the celebrations. The sailors were dancing up on the deck, and when the young prince appeared, a hundred rockets shot up into the sky and turned the night back into bright day.

The little mermaid was quite scared and ducked back beneath the water, but she soon surfaced again. It felt as if the stars were falling out of the sky. She had never seen such fireworks. Great suns were spinning around, fiery fish were darting about the blue air, and all this glitter was reflected back from the clear mirror of the sea. The deck of the ship was so brightly lit that you could see every rope. How handsome the young prince was! He was laughing and smiling and

shaking hands with everyone, while music rang out into the night.

It grew late, but the little mermaid could not take her eyes from the ship, and the handsome prince. The lanterns were put out; the rockets were finished; no more cannons were fired. Yet deep beneath the sea there was a murmuring and grumbling. Still the mermaid rocked up and down on the waves to look into the cabin.

The ship gathered speed; more sails were unfurled. The waves became choppy, and clouds began to mass; in the distance there were flashes of lightning. A storm was brewing.

The sails were taken in, and the ship was tossed about by the huge waves that rose like black mountains high above the masts. The ship was like a swan diving down into the troughs of the waves and riding high on their crests. The little mermaid watched it all with glee—she thought it was great fun. But it was no joke for the sailors. The ship creaked and cracked, and its stout timbers shivered as the raging sea pounded against them. Suddenly the main mast snapped like a stick, and then the ship keeled over on her side as water poured into the hold.

Now the little mermaid could see that they were in danger; she herself had to watch out for planks and bits of wreckage that were floating in the water. For a moment it was so dark she couldn't see a thing; then lightning flashed and she could make out all the figures on board. It was every man for himself. She looked desperately for the young prince, and caught sight of him just as the ship broke up and sank into the sea. For a split second she was filled with joy. Now he was coming to her! But then she remembered that men cannot live in the water, and that he could only come to her father's palace as a corpse.

No! He must not die! She flung herself forward, heedless of the drifting beams that might have crushed her, plunging into the turbulent waves again and again until she found the prince. He was barely able to keep afloat in that heaving sea; his arms and legs were tired out. He closed his beautiful eyes, and he must certainly have drowned if the little mermaid had not come to him. She held his head above water and let the waves carry the two of them where they would.

By morning the storm was over. Not a trace of the ship remained. The sun rose up red and glorious from the waves, and it seemed to bring a touch of life to the pale face of the prince, though his eyes remained shut. The mermaid kissed his forehead and stroked his wet hair. She thought he looked like the marble statue in her garden. She kissed him again, and wished with all her heart that he might live.

Now she could see dry land ahead, and high blue mountains with snow-covered peaks. Down by the shore there were green woods and a little whitewashed church or monastery, the little mermaid didn't know which. Orange and lemon trees grew in the garden, and by the gate were tall palms. There was a little bay with deep water right up to the shore, and the mermaid swam into it with the handsome prince and laid him on the white sand in the sun, taking care that his head was out of the water.

Now bells rang out from the building, and some young girls came out to walk in the garden. So the little mermaid swam out to some foam-flecked rocks and hid behind them, so that she could wait for someone to come and help the poor prince.

Quite soon a young girl came by. She seemed startled to see the half-drowned figure, but only for a few seconds; then she went and fetched help. The mermaid saw the prince revive and smile at those around him. He did not smile at her; he did not even know that she had rescued him. She felt empty. After he had been taken into the white building, she dived down into the water and returned sorrowing to her father's palace.

She had always been quiet and thoughtful; now she was even more so. Her sisters asked her what she had seen on her first visit to the surface, but she wouldn't say.

On many evenings, and many mornings, she went back to the place where she had left the prince. She saw the fruits in the garden grow ripe and be harvested. She saw the snow melt from the mountaintops, but she never saw the prince, and so she always went home even sadder than before.

Her one comfort was to sit in her little garden with her arms wrapped around the beautiful marble statue that reminded her so much of the prince. She never tended the flowers, and they grew wild and tangled, climbing and interweaving until they shut out all the light from the garden.

At last she could bear it no longer and told one of her sisters her story; so before long all the sisters knew about it—but nobody else, except for a few mermaids who only told their closest friends. And it was one of these who found out who the prince was. She too had seen the birthday party on the ship, and she knew where he came from and where his kingdom lay.

"Come on, little sister," said the other princesses, and with their arms twined around each other's shoulders they rose up through the sea to surface outside the prince's palace.

The palace was built of pale yellow stone, with great flights of marble steps, one of which stretched right down to the sea. Gilded domes capped the roof, and between the pillars around the building were lifelike marble statues. Through the clear glass of the high windows you could see right into the state apartments with their precious hangings and tapestries and wonderful paintings. In the middle of the biggest room a great fountain played, splashing its water right up to a glass dome in the roof. The sun shone down through the glass onto the fountain and the beautiful plants that grew in it.

Now that she knew where he lived, she went there many an evening and many a night. She swam closer than any of the others dared—right up the narrow canal into the shadow cast by the prince's marble balcony. There she would gaze at the young prince, who believed himself all alone in the moonlight.

Often in the evening she saw him sailing in his fine boat, with its banners flying and music playing. She peeped from behind the reeds on the shore, and if anyone caught sight of her long silver veil when it was caught by the breeze, they only thought it was a swan flirting its wings.

Many a time, later at night, when the fishermen were casting their nets by torchlight, she heard them speaking well of the young prince, and that made her glad, for she had saved his life when he lay drifting half-dead on the waves. She remembered how his head had rested on her breast, and how fiercely she had kissed him. But he knew nothing about that; he never dreamed she existed.

She became fonder and fonder of human beings, and longed to join them. Their world seemed so much larger than hers. They could sail across the oceans in ships, and climb mountains high above the clouds. Their lands with their fields and forests seemed to stretch forever. There was so much she wanted to know; questions her sisters couldn't answer. So she quizzed her old grandmother for everything she knew about the upper world, as she called the countries above the sea.

"If human beings are not drowned, do they live forever?" she asked. "Or do they die, as we do in the sea?"

"Yes," said the old lady, "they must die. And their lives are far shorter than ours. We can live for three hundred years, but at the end we just turn to foam on the water—we do not even have a grave down here among our loved ones. We do not have immortal souls; there is no new life for us. We're like the green reeds—once they are cut, they will never be green again. But human beings have a soul which lives forever, even after their body has turned to dust. The soul rises through the air to the bright stars. Just as we rise up out of the sea and gaze on the upper world, so they rise up to unknown glorious regions that we shall never see."

"Why have we no immortal soul?" the little mermaid asked sadly. "I would give all my three hundred years if I could live as a human being for one single day, and share in that heavenly world."

"You must not think of such things," said her grandmother. "We are happier and better off here than they are up there."

"So I shall die, and drift as foam upon the ocean," said the little mermaid, "and never hear the waves again, or see the lovely flowers and the red sun. Is there nothing I can do to gain an immortal soul?"

"No," said the old lady. "Only if a human loved you more than his father and mother, and thought only of you, and let a priest take his right hand and put it in yours, while he promised to be true to you for all eternity, then his soul would flow into you, and you would share in human happiness. He would give you a soul, yet still keep his own. But that can never be. For what we think beautiful down here—your tail—is thought ugly up there. They prefer two clumsy props, called legs."

The little mermaid glanced down at her fishtail, and sighed.

"We must be content with what we have," said the old lady, "and make the best of our three hundred years. We should dance and be gay; for it's a long sleep after. Tonight, let's have a court ball!"

It was a magnificent affair, the like of which has never been seen on earth. The walls and ceilings of the great ballroom were made of glass—quite thick, but perfectly clear. Several hundred enormous shells, rose red and grass green, were ranged as lamps on either side, and their blue flames lit up the whole room. Light spilled through the glass walls into the sea outside, where countless fish could be seen swimming about, their scales glowing purple, silver, and gold.

Through the middle of the ballroom flowed a broad swift stream, on which the sea folk danced to their own sweet songs. No humans have such lovely voices, and the little mermaid sang most beautifully of all. The others clapped their hands for her, and for a moment she felt a thrill of joy, for knew that she had the most beautiful voice of anyone on land or sea. But her thoughts soon returned to the world above, for she could not forget the handsome prince and her grief that she did not, like him, have an immortal soul. So she crept out of her father's palace, and while everyone else danced and sang, she sat alone in her gloomy little garden.

From up above she heard the sound of a horn echoing through the water. *There he is,* she thought, *sailing so far beyond my reach, though I love him more than my father and mother, though he is always in my thoughts, though I would place my life's happiness in his hands.*

To win his love, and gain an immortal soul, I would dare anything! While my sisters are dancing in the palace, I will go to the sea witch, though I have always feared her, and ask her to help me.

And so the little mermaid left her garden and swam to the place where the sea witch lived, on the far side of a raging whirlpool. She had never gone that way before. No flowers grew there; no sea grass; nothing but bare sand until she reached the fearsome whirlpool, which was twisting and turning like a millwheel, dragging everything it could clutch down into the deep. She had to brave those roaring waters to reach the sea witch's domain. Once through the whirlpool, the path lay over a swamp of hot, bubbling mud, which the sea witch called her peat bog. Beyond this lay the witch's house, deep in an eerie forest.

The trees and bushes in this forest were all what they call polyps—half beast and half plant. They looked like hundred-headed snakes growing from the ground. Their branches were long slimy arms with fingers like wiggling worms; they never stopped moving, from root to tip, and whatever they touched they wound round, never to let go.

The little mermaid paused at the edge of this wood. She was so frightened she thought her heart would stop beating. She almost turned back. But then she thought of the prince, and the human soul, and that gave her courage. She bound up her long flowing hair, so that the polyps could not snatch at it. Then she folded her hands together and dived forward, darting as fast as the fastest fish, in and out of the gruesome branches, which reached out their waving arms after her. She noticed that every one of them was holding tight to something it had caught: white skulls of drowned men, ships' rudders and seamen's chests, skeletons of land animals, and—most horrible of all—a little mermaid whom they had taken and throttled.

Now she came to a swampy clearing in the wood, where enormous eels were writhing about, exposing their gross, sallow underbellies. Here the witch had built her house from the bones of shipwrecked men, and here she sat, letting a toad feed out of her mouth, just as some people do with a pet canary. She called the vile, slimy eels her little chickabiddies, and pressed them close to her great spongy chest.

"I know what you're after," she cackled, "and you're a fool. But you shall have your wish, for it will only bring you misery, my pretty princess. You want to be rid of your fishtail, and have two stumps instead, like humans have, and then the prince will fall in love with you, and you will marry him, and win an immortal soul—isn't that so?" And the sea witch gave such an evil laugh that the toad and the eels fell away from her and lay there sprawling in the slime.

"You've come in the nick of time," said the witch. "Tomorrow I couldn't have helped you for another year. I shall prepare you a potion. Tomorrow morning go to the shore and drink it before the sun rises. Then your tail will split in two, and shrink into what humans call 'pretty legs.' But it will hurt. It will be like a sharp sword slicing through you. Everyone who sees you will say you are the loveliest girl they have ever seen. But though you will move with a dancer's grace, every step you take will be like treading on a sharp knife—a blade that cuts to the bone. Will you suffer all this? If so, I can help you."

"Yes," said the little mermaid, though her voice trembled. She fixed her thoughts on the prince, and the prize of an immortal soul.

"Don't forget," said the witch, "when once you have taken a human shape, you can never again be a mermaid. You can never dive down to your father's place, or to your sisters. Yet if you do not win the prince's love, so that he forgets his father and mother and thinks only of you, and lets the priest join your hands as man and wife, then you will get no immortal soul. On the morning after the prince marries another, your heart will break and you will be nothing but foam on the water."

"My mind is made up," said the little mermaid, as pale as death.

"Then there's the matter of my fee," said the witch. "I won't do it for nothing. Yours is the most beautiful voice of all the sea folk; I expect you think to use it to charm the prince. But that voice you must give to me. You must pay for my potion with the most precious thing you possess. For in return I must shed my own blood, to make the potion as sharp as a two-edged sword."

"But if you take my voice," said the little mermaid, "what will I have left?"

"Your beauty, your grace, and your speaking eyes," said the witch. "These are enough to win a human heart. Well? Have you lost your courage? Put out your little tongue, and I shall cut it off in payment; then you shall receive my precious potion."

"Let it be so," said the little mermaid.

The witch put a cauldron on the fire to prepare her potion. "Cleanliness is a good thing," she said, wiping out the cauldron with some eels that she had tied into a knot. Then she scratched her breast and let black blood drip into the cauldron. The steam that arose was full of terrifying shapes. Every moment the witch threw some dread ingredient into the brew. When it came to the boil, it made the sound of a crying crocodile. But when the potion was ready, it looked like the clearest water.

"There you are!" said the witch, and she cut off the little mermaid's tongue. Now she had no voice, and she could neither sing nor speak.

"If the polyps give you any trouble on the way back," said the witch, "just throw one single drop of this potion at them, and they will split apart." But there was no need for that. When the polyps saw her, they shrank back in terror from the bright vial shining in her hand like a

star. So the little mermaid passed safely back across the wood, the swamp, and the roaring whirlpool.

She could see her father's palace. The lights were out in the great ballroom; everyone must be asleep. She didn't dare go and look, now that she had lost her voice and was going to leave them for ever. She felt her heart would break from grief. She crept into the garden and took one flower from the flower beds of each of her sisters; then she blew them each a farewell kiss, and rose up through the deep blue sea.

The sun had not yet risen when she reached the prince's castle and made her way up the marble steps. The moon shone bright and clear. The little mermaid drank the bitter, burning drink, and it was as if a two-edged sword had been thrust through her delicate body. She fainted away with the pain.

When the sun's rays touched her she awoke. The pain was still as sharp, but there in front of her stood the young prince. He fastened his jet-black eyes on her, and she cast her eyes down—and then she saw that her fishtail was gone, and that instead she had the prettiest, slenderest legs that any girl could wish for. But she was quite naked, so she wrapped herself in her long flowing hair.

The prince asked who she was and how she had come there, but she could only look at him with her sweet, sad eyes; she could not speak. He took her by the hand and led her into the palace. Just as the witch had warned her, every step was like treading on a knife-edge. But she welcomed the pain. With her hand in the prince's, she felt she was walking on air. Everyone who saw her was charmed by her grace of movement.

She was given a lovely dress of silk and muslin, and everyone agreed she was the most beautiful girl in the palace. But she was mute, and could neither sing nor speak.

Beautiful girls dressed in silk and gold came and performed for the prince and his parents. One of them sang more prettily than the rest, and the prince clapped his hands and smiled at her. It made the little mermaid sad, for she knew that she had once sung far more beautifully. And she thought, *Oh! If only he knew I had sacrificed my voice in order to be with him!*

Next the girls did a delightful dance. When they had finished, the little mermaid lifted her arms and stood on the tips of her toes. Then she began to float across the dance floor, with a grace that had never been seen before. There was such beauty in her movements, and her eyes were so full of feeling, that everyone was enchanted—especially the prince. He called her his little foundling. So she danced on and on, though every time her foot touched the floor she felt she was treading on sharp knives. The prince declared she must never leave him, and she was given a place to sleep outside his door on a velvet cushion.

The prince had a boy's velvet suit made for her, so that she could ride out with him on horseback. They rode through the sweet-smelling woods, where green branches brushed their shoulders, and the little birds trilled from among the cool leaves. She climbed high hills by the prince's side, and though her delicate feet bled for all to see, she only laughed, and followed him until they could see the clouds sailing beneath them like a flock of birds setting off for distant lands.

At night in the palace, while the others slept, she would go down the marble steps and cool her poor burning feet in the cold water. Then she would think of her sisters, down in the deep sea.

One night they came, arm in arm, singing the saddest song. She waved to them, and they recognized her at once. They told her how unhappy she had made them all. After that, they visited every night. Once she saw her old grandmother, far out to sea, and once her father, the sea king, with his crown on his head. They stretched out their hands to her, but they did not venture near enough to speak.

Day by day the prince grew more fond of her. But he loved her only as a dear, good child—he never thought of making her his wife. And she had to become his wife, or she could never win an immortal soul. On the day he married another, she would dissolve into foam on the sea.

"Don't you love me best?" her eyes would plead, when he took her in his arms and kissed her lovely brow.

"You really are the dearest creature," the prince would say, "because you have the kindest heart. You are so devoted, and you remind me of a young girl I saw only once, and shall probably never see again. I was on a ship that was wrecked, and the waves carried me to land close to a convent, which was home to many young maidens. The youngest of them all found me on the beach and saved my life. I saw her but twice, no more, yet I know she is the only one I could ever love, and you are so like her that you almost take her place in my heart. She belongs to the temple, but good fortune has sent you to me—we shall never be parted!"

Ah! He does not know that I was the one who saved his life, thought the little mermaid. *He does not know that I was the one who carried him through the waves to the convent, or that I waited in the foam to see if anyone would come, and saw the pretty girl whom he loves better than me.* She gave a deep sigh, for she did not know how to cry. *The girl belongs to the convent; so she will never come out into the world. I am with him every day. I will care for him, and love him, and give up my life to him.*

But now people said that the young prince was to be married. He was fitting out a fine ship to go and see the country of another king, but everyone said, "It's not the country, it's the princess he's going to inspect." The little mermaid just shook her head and smiled a secret smile, for she knew the prince's thoughts, and they didn't.

"I shall have to go," he told her. "My parents insist. But they cannot make me marry this princess, however pretty she is. I cannot love her. She will not remind me of the beautiful girl in the temple, as you do. If ever I chose a bride, I should choose you first, my silent foundling with the speaking eyes!" And he kissed her rose-red mouth, played with her long hair, and laid his head so near her heart that she was filled with dreams of human happiness and an immortal soul.

"Have you no fear of the sea, my silent child?" he said, as they stood on the deck of the splendid ship that was to take him to the nearby kingdom. He told the little mermaid how the sea could turn in a moment from calm to storm, and of the rare fish in the deep, and the strange sights divers had seen down there. And she smiled at his tales, for she knew better than he what lay beneath the waves.

In the moonlit night, when everyone but the helmsman at the wheel was asleep, she sat on the ship's rail and stared down through the clear water. She thought she saw her father's palace. On the topmost tower her grandmother was perched, with a silver crown on her head, staring up through the swift current at the passing ship. Then her sisters came to the surface, wringing their white hands, and looking at her with despair. She waved to them and smiled; she wanted them to know that all was well with her. But just then the cabin boy came out, and her sisters dived down; all he saw was foam on the water.

Next morning the ship sailed into port. Church bells rang out, and soldiers stood to attention with glittering bayonets. Banners were flying; everyone was on holiday. The prince was invited to one ball or party after another; but nothing was seen of the princess. It was said that she was being educated at a convent, learning how to be royal.

At last she arrived. The little mermaid was waiting for her, eager to judge her beauty. She had to admit that it would be hard to find a lovelier human girl. Her skin was so clear and delicate, and behind long dark lashes she had a pair of baby blue eyes.

"It is you!" cried the prince. "You who saved me when I lay half dead on the shore." And he clasped the blushing princess in his arms.

"Now I am too happy," he told the little mermaid. "My dearest wish—all I ever dared hope for—has been granted. You, whose heart is so true, will share my happiness." And the little mermaid kissed his hand and thought her heart would break. His wedding morning would bring her death; she would be nothing but foam on the sea.

All the church bells rang, and heralds rode through the streets to announce the wedding.

On the altar, silver lamps burned rare oils. The priests swung censers with burning incense. The prince and princess gave each other their hands, and the bishop blessed them. The little mermaid, dressed in silk and gold, held up the train of the bride's dress. But her ears did not hear the music, and her eyes did not see the sacred ceremony. This night would bring her death, and she was thinking of all she had lost.

That evening, the bride and bridegroom went on board ship; cannons were fired, and banners flew. Right on the main deck, a sumptuous tent of scarlet and gold had been set up, with the softest cushions on which the happy pair would rest on that calm, cool night.

The sails swelled in the breeze, and the ship glided across the clear water.

As darkness fell, bright lamps were lit, and the sailors danced jigs and reels on the deck. The little mermaid remembered the first time she had come to the surface, and had spied on just such a scene. Now she, too, whirled in the dance, gliding and soaring as a swallow does when it is pursued. How everyone cheered and clapped! Never before had she danced with such abandon. Sharp knives sliced her tender feet, but she scarcely felt the pain beside the raw wound in her heart. This was the last time she would see him—the handsome prince for whom she had given up her beautiful voice, turned her back on her home and family, and day after day endured pain without end. He had never noticed any of it.This was the last time she would breathe the same air as he, or look upon the deep sea or the starry sky. An everlasting night, without thoughts, without dreams, awaited her—for she had no soul, nor any hope of one.

The merrymaking lasted long into the night. The little mermaid danced and laughed, with the thought of death heavy in her heart. Then the prince kissed his lovely bride, she caressed his dark locks, and arm in arm they retired to their magnificent tent.

The ship was hushed and still; there was only the helmsman standing at the wheel. The little mermaid leaned her white arms on the rail and looked eastward for the first pink of dawn. The first ray of sun, she knew, would kill her.

Then she saw her sisters rising out of the water. Their faces were pale and grim, and their long lustrous hair no longer streamed in the wind—it had been cut off.

"We have given our hair to the sea witch, so that she would help us to save your life. She has given us this knife. See how sharp it is! Before the sun rises you must plunge it into the prince's heart. When his warm blood splashes over your feet they will join together into a fishtail, and you will be a mermaid once more. You can come down to us and live out your three hundred years before you melt into the salt sea foam. Hurry! Either he or you must die by sunrise. Our old grandmother is grieving; her white hair has fallen out through sorrow, just as ours fell before the scissors of the witch. Kill the prince, and come back to us! Hurry! Do you not see the red streak in the sky? In a few minutes the sun will rise, and then you must die." And with a strange, deep sigh they sank beneath the waves.

The little mermaid drew aside the purple curtain of the tent and saw the beautiful bride asleep, with her head on the prince's breast. She stooped and kissed his handsome brow, glanced into the sky where the red light of dawn was glowing ever stronger, and looked back to the prince. In his sleep he was calling his bride by name; she alone filled his thoughts. The knife trembled in the mermaid's hand.

She flung it far out to sea. There was a glimmer of red as it fell, as if red drops of blood were splashing up from the water. One last glimpse of the prince through eyes half glazed by death, and she threw herself into the sea; she felt her body dissolving into the foam.

And now the sun came rising from the sea. It rays were so gentle and warm on the cold foam that the little mermaid did not feel the hand of death. She saw the bright sun and, hovering above her, hundreds of bright transparent creatures—she could see through them to the white sails of the ship and the pink clouds in the sky. Their voices were pure melody—so pure that no human ear could hear it, just as no human eye could see them. They had no wings—they were lighter than air. The little mermaid saw that she had become like them, and was floating free above the foam.

"Who are you?" she asked, and she had a voice again—a voice like theirs, so heavenly that no music could ever capture it.

"We are the daughters of the air!" they replied. "A mermaid has no immortal soul, and she can never gain one unless she wins the love of a mortal. Her only chance of eternal life depends upon another. We daughters of the air are not given an immortal soul either, but by good deeds we can make our own soul. We fly to the hot countries, where plague gathers in the sultry air, and blow cool breezes to dispel it. We carry the healing fragrance of flowers to the sick. If for three hundred years we do nothing but good, then we win an immortal soul, and a share in mankind's eternal happiness. You, poor little mermaid, have striven with all your heart. You have suffered, and endured, and have raised yourself into the world of the spirits of the air. Now, by three hundred years of good deeds, you can make yourself an immortal soul."

And the little mermaid raised her translucent arms to the sun, and for the first time she shed a tear.

She heard life and movement from the ship. The prince and the princess were searching for her; they were gazing sadly into the foam, as if they guessed she had flung herself into the sea. Unseen, she kissed the bride's forehead, gave a smile to the prince, and then with the other daughters of the air she ascended to a rose-pink cloud that was sailing by.

"In three hundred years I shall rise like this into the kingdom of heaven," she whispered.

"Maybe even sooner," said one of the others. "We enter unseen into human homes where there are children. Whenever we find a good child, who makes its parents happy and repays their love, it makes us smile with joy, and a year is taken from the three hundred. But if we see a mean and naughty child, then we must weep tears of sorrow, and every tear adds another day to our time of trial."

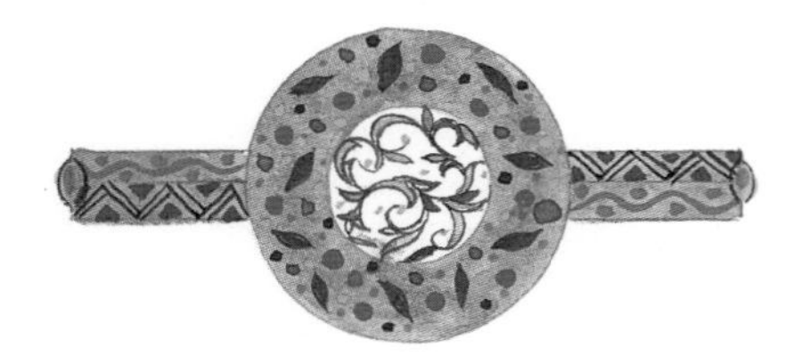

THE EMPEROR'S NEW CLOTHES

MANY years ago there was an emperor who was so mad about fashionable new clothes that he spent all his money on dressing up. He never inspected his army, or went to the theatre, or drove through the countryside, unless he had a new outfit to show off. He had different clothes for every hour of the day, and at any time when you might say of another king, "His Majesty is in the council chamber," you could always say of him, "The emperor's in his dressing room."

The emperor's city was a hive of activity, and there were always strangers coming and going. One day a pair of swindlers turned up, claiming to be weavers. Their cloth, they boasted, was not just of the finest quality and design, but had the virtue of being invisible to anyone who was stupid or not fit to hold his job.

What wonderful cloth! thought the emperor. *If I wore it, I would be able to find out which of my courtiers are unfit for their posts, and also be able to tell the clever ones from the stupid. Yes, I must have a suit made at once!* He handed over a large sum of money to the swindlers, so that they could start work straight away.

So the swindlers set up a loom and pretended to be weaving, though in fact there was nothing at all on their loom. They coolly demanded the finest silks and costliest gold thread, which they stuffed into their own packs, and then carried on working at the empty loom into the night.

I wonder how they're getting on with my cloth, thought the emperor. But there was one thing which made him feel uneasy, and that was that a man who was stupid or unfit for his job would not be able to see the cloth. Not that *he* had anything to fear, but all the same he thought it might be best to send someone else first to see how things were going. Everyone in the city had heard about the special virtue of the cloth, and they were all agog to find out how stupid or incompetent their friends were.

I will send my honest old prime minister to the weavers, thought the emperor. *He'll be the best judge of the cloth, for he's got brains, and he's good at his job.*

So the honest old prime minister went to the room where the two swindlers were working away. *Good Lord!* thought the old man, as he goggled at the empty loom. *I can't see a thing!* But he kept that to himself.

The swindlers begged him to be so good as to come closer and tell them what he thought of the cloth. "Do you like the design?" They pointed to the empty loom, but though the poor old man stared and stared he couldn't see a thing. *Oh dear!* he thought. *Does this mean that I am stupid? I never had an inkling, and no one else must either! Or perhaps I am unfit for my job? Whatever, no one must find out that I cannot see the cloth.*

"Now, do you like it or not?" asked one of the weavers.

"Oh, it's charming, absolutely delightful," said the old prime minister, peering through his spectacles. "What a gorgeous pattern! I shall tell the emperor that I am most pleased with it."

"You're too kind," said the swindlers. And then they described the pattern in detail, and the old prime minister listened carefully so that he could repeat it all to the emperor—which he duly did.

The swindlers now asked for more money, silk, and gold thread, in order to finish the cloth. But it all went straight into their own pockets. Not a single thread was put on the loom—they just carried on weaving air.

Before long, the emperor sent a second offical to see how work was progressing, and find out when the clothes would be ready. The same things happened to him as to the prime minister. No matter how hard he looked, he could not see anything on the empty loom.

"It's really beautiful, isn't it?" asked one of the swindlers.

I'm not stupid, thought the official, *so I must be unfit for my job. If people found out, I'd be a laughingstock.* So he too praised the material which he couldn't see, and said how pleased he was with its subtle shades and beautiful design.

"It's quite exquisite," he told the emperor.

The wonderful material was the talk of the town. At last, the emperor decided he must go and see it for himself while it was still on the loom. He took along a number of courtiers, including the two honest officials who had already described the cloth, to see the two swindlers working busily at their empty looms.

"Isn't it *magnifique?*" said the two honest officials. "Just look at the pattern, Your Majesty." And they pointed to the empty loom, sure that everyone else could see the cloth.

What's this? thought the emperor. *I can't see anything! Am I stupid? Or am I unfit to be emperor? This is too awful for words.* "Oh! It's wonderful!" he said. "It is everything I hoped for." And he gave a satisfied nod at the empty loom. He wasn't going to admit he couldn't see a thing.

All the others who were there were in the same boat. They could see nothing, but they all said what the emperor said: "Oh! It's wonderful!" They told him he should have some clothes made from the magnificent material in time to wear them at the great procession that was soon to take place. "Magnificent! Wonderful! Superb!" were the words on everyone's lips. They were all delighted. The emperor gave each of the swindlers a knighthood, with a medal to wear in his buttonhole, and the title "knight of the loom."

The swindlers sat up all night before the procession, with more than sixteen candles burning, so that people could see how hard they were working on the emperor's new clothes. They pretended to take the cloth off the loom, made cuts in the air with huge scissors, and sewed with needles that had no thread, and finally they announced, "Look! The emperor's clothes are ready!"

The emperor came with his courtiers, and the weavers held out their arms as if they were carrying something, and said, "Here are the trousers! Here is the jacket! Here is the cloak!" and so on. "The whole suit is as light as a spider's web. You'll feel as if you've got nothing on; that's the beauty of the cloth."

"Yes indeed!" said all the courtiers; but they couldn't see anything, for there was nothing to see.

"If Your Majesty would graciously take off the clothes you are wearing, we shall think it a privilege to help you into the new ones in front of the great mirror."

So the emperor took off all his clothes, and the swindlers went through the motions of fitting him with his new suit, even pretending to fasten the train around his waist. The emperor turned this way and that, preening in the mirror.

"How elegant Your Majesty looks! What a perfect fit!" everyone exclaimed. "What a triumph!"

Then the master of ceremonies announced, "The canopy which will be carried above Your Majesty in the procession is waiting outside."

"I am ready to go," said the emperor. "See how well my new clothes fit!" And he did a final twirl in front of the mirror, pretending to admire his fine clothes.

The chamberlains, who were to carry the emperor's train, fumbled on the floor looking for it. They didn't dare admit they couldn't see anything, so they pretended to pick the train up, and as they walked they held their hands in the air as if they were carrying it.

So the emperor marched in procession under the beautiful canopy, and all the people lining the streets or standing at their windows exclaimed, "The emperor's new clothes are the best he's ever had! What a perfect fit! And just look at the train!" For no one wanted

people to think that he couldn't see anything, and so was a fool, or unfit for his job. Never had the emperor's clothes been such a success.

"But he hasn't got anything on!" said a little child.

"Listen to the little innocent!" said the father.

But the whisper passed through the crowd: "He hasn't got anything on! There's a little child who says he hasn't got anything on!" And at last the people shouted with one voice, "He hasn't got anything on!"

The emperor had the uncomfortable feeling that they were right. But he thought, *I must go through with it now.* So he drew himself up to his full height and walked proudly on, and the chamberlains walked behind him carrying the train that wasn't there.

THE STEADFAST TIN SOLDIER

ONCE there were twenty-five soldiers, all brothers, because they were all made out of the same old tin spoon. They stood up straight with their muskets on their shoulders, very proud in their red and blue uniforms. The very first thing they heard in the world, when the lid of their box was taken off, was "Tin soldiers!" It was a little boy who shouted it, with a clap of his hands. They were a birthday present, and he paraded them on the table.

All the soldiers were exactly alike, except one. He'd only got one leg, because he was made last, and the tin had run out. But he stood just as firm on his one leg as the others did on two, and he's the one this story is about.

There were plenty of other toys on the table where the tin soldiers were set out, but the one that really caught your eye was a paper castle. You could see through its little windows right into the rooms. Outside, tiny trees stood beside a little mirror, which was meant to be a lake. Wax swans swam on it, admiring their own reflections.

It was a lovely scene—and loveliest of all was the girl who stood in the castle's open door. She too was cut out of paper, but her skirt was made of finest muslin, and as a shawl around her shoulders she wore a narrow sky-blue ribbon, fastened with a gleaming star the size of her face. She stretched out her arms, for she was a dancer, and kicked one leg so high that the tin soldier couldn't see it, and thought she'd only got one leg, like him.

"That's just the wife for me," he thought. "But she's so grand. She lives in a castle. I have only a box, and there are twenty-five of us in that. There's no room for her. Still, I'll try to get to know her." So he hid behind a snuff box that was on the table, where he had a good view of the charming dancer, poised with such perfect balance on one leg.

When night came, the other tin soldiers were put back in their box, and the children went to bed. Now it was time for the toys to play. They paid each other visits, waged wars, and even held a ball. How the tin soldiers rattled in their box, trying to join in! But they couldn't get the lid off. The nutcracker turned somersaults, and the slate pencil kept score on the slate. They made such a row they woke the canary, and it started speechifying—in verse, too!

Only two never moved. The little dancer stayed on tiptoe with her arms outstretched, and the tin soldier stood steadfast on his single leg, and his eyes never left her for a moment.

And then the clock struck twelve, and *crash!* up jumped the lid of the snuff box. There wasn't any snuff inside, oh no. Out sprang a little black goblin. It was a Jack-in-the-box.

"Tin soldier!" said the goblin. "You keep your eyes to yourself." But the tin soldier pretended not to hear.

"All right," said the goblin. "Just you wait till tomorrow."

And whether it was the goblin's doing or just the wind, no one can say, but next morning, when the children got up, and the little boy put the tin soldier on the windowsill, the window flew open and the tin soldier fell, head over heels, from three floors up. It was a fearful drop. He landed on his head with his leg in the air and his bayonet trapped between two cobblestones.

The maid and the little boy went to look for him there and then, but even though they nearly trod on him they didn't see him. If only he had called out, "Here I am!" they would have found him, but he didn't think it right to make a commotion when he was wearing his uniform.

Now it began to rain, heavier and heavier till it was a real storm. And when it was over, along came two street kids.

"Look!" said one. "Here's a tin soldier! Let's sail him."

So they made a boat out of newspaper and put the tin soldier in it, and away he sailed down the gutter, with the boys running by his side clapping their hands. Heavens above! What waves, what tides there were in that gutter. It had been a real downpour.

The boat plunged up and down and whirled round and round till the tin soldier was quite dizzy. But he stood fast. He never flinched, but looked straight ahead with his musket on his shoulder.

Suddenly the boat ducked into a gutter pipe. It was as dark in there as in his box at home.

"Where am I going now?" he wondered. "Oh, it's all that goblin's fault. But if only the little dancer was by my side, I wouldn't care if it was twice as dark."

Just then a huge rat, who lived in the pipe, darted out. "Passport!" said the rat. "Where's your passport?"

The tin soldier kept quiet and gripped his musket. The boat sailed on and the rat gave chase. Ugh! How he gnashed his teeth, screeching to floating bits of straw and wood, "Stop him! Stop him! He's not paid the toll! He hasn't shown his passport!"

But the current swept faster and faster. The tin soldier could already spy daylight at the end of the pipe, but he could also hear a terrible roaring fit to frighten the bravest of men. Think of it: at the end of the pipe, the water gushed out into a great canal. It was as risky for him as it would be for us to plunge down a mighty waterfall.

He was so near there was no stopping. The boat raced out, and the poor tin soldier braced himself as stiffly as he could; no one could say he so much as blinked.

The boat spun round three or four times and filled with water to the brim. It had to sink. The tin soldier was in the water up to his neck. Down, down sank the boat. The paper turned to mush, and the water

closed over the tin soldier's head. He thought of the lovely little dancer whom he would never see again, and the words of an old song rang in his ears:

March on, march on to victory—
Tomorrow you must die.

The boat fell to bits, the soldier fell through—and at that very moment was swallowed up by a great fish.

Oh my! How dark it was in there! It was even worse than the gutter pipe, and a tighter fit, too. But the tin soldier was steadfast. He lay there, flat out, with his musket over his shoulder. Round and about swam the fish, with all sorts of twists and turns. Then it was still. Then, a bolt of lightning seemed to flash through it. It was the clear light of day, and someone was exclaiming, "A tin soldier!" For the fish had been caught, and taken to market, and sold, and now it was in the kitchen where the cook had cut it open with a big knife.

She picked up the tin soldier round the waist, and carried him between her finger and thumb into the living room. Everyone wanted to see the remarkable character who had voyaged inside a fish. But the tin soldier didn't let it go to his head.

They stood him on the table and—the world is full of wonders—there he was, back in the very room he'd set out from.

Here were the same children, the same toys on the table, the beautiful castle, the graceful little dancer. Still she balanced on just one leg, with the other held high in the air. She, too, was steadfast. The tin soldier was touched to the quick. He could have wept tin tears, if he hadn't been a soldier. He looked at her, and she looked at him, but they never said a word.

Suddenly, the little boy took the soldier and flung him into the stove. Why, he couldn't say. No doubt the goblin in the snuff box was at the bottom of it.

The tin soldier stood in a blaze of light. Whether he burned from the heat of the fire or the heat of his love he did not know. All his paint was gone; whether from the hardships of his journey or the bitterness of his grief, no one could tell.

He looked at the little dancer and she looked at him. He felt himself melting away, but he was steadfast, with his musket on his shoulder. Then the door opened, a draft caught the dancer, and she flew into the stove to the tin soldier. She flared and was gone. And then the tin soldier melted back into a lump of tin.

Next morning, when she raked out the ashes, the maid found him, shaped like a little tin heart. Of the dancer nothing remained, save the star from her breast, and that was burned as black as coal.

THE FLYING TRUNK

ONCE there was a merchant who was so rich that he could have paved the whole street with silver. But he didn't actually do that because he had other ideas about what to do with his money. Before he spent a copper coin, he made sure he would get a silver one back. That's the sort of merchant he was. A merchant he lived, and a merchant he died.

All his money now went to his son, who had a high old time with it. He went dancing every night, made paper kites out of folding money, and skimmed gold pieces over the lake instead of stones. That's the way the money goes, and it did. Soon he had nothing left but four pennies, a pair of slippers, and an old dressing gown. His friends wouldn't have anything more to do with him; they didn't want to be seen with him on the street. But one of them, in a friendly spirit, sent him an old trunk, with the advice, "Get packing!"

A fat lot of good that was—he didn't have anything to pack. So he packed himself.

It was a strange trunk. As soon as you pressed the lock, it took off into the air. And that's what it did now! Up it flew, with the young man in it, up the chimney, through the clouds, and off into the wild blue yonder.

The bottom of the trunk kept creaking, and the young man was scared it would fall to bits—and then, heaven help me, he'd have had to learn some fancy acrobatics fast. But at last he landed in Turkey.

He hid the trunk in the woods and walked into town. He felt right at home, as the Turks all went around just like him in dressing gowns and slippers. Then he met a nurse with a baby. "Nurse," he said, "what is that big palace over there, with the high windows?"

"That is where the princess lives," she replied. "It has been foretold that she will be unlucky in love, so no one is allowed to visit her unless the king and queen are there."

"Thank you," said the merchant's son, and he went back to the wood, got into his trunk, flew up to the palace roof, and crept in at the princess's window.

She was lying on her sofa asleep. She was so lovely that the merchant's son couldn't stop himself from kissing her. This woke her up, and she was scared out of her wits until he told her he was a god, who had come down to her from the sky. That cheered her up.

They sat side by side on the sofa, and he told her stories about her eyes. They were like dark deep lakes, he said, in which her thoughts swam like lovely mermaids. He told her about her forehead—it was like a snowy mountain, with wonderful caves full of treasure. And he told her about the stork, which brings dear little babies. Oh, he said wonderful things. So when he asked her to marry him, she said yes.

"Come back on Saturday," she said, "and have tea with the king and queen. They will be so proud when I tell them that I am going to marry a god. They love stories, so you must be sure to have a good one to tell them. My mother likes high-class stories with a proper moral, and my father likes funny ones that makes him laugh."

"I shall bring a story as my wedding gift," he said. Before they parted, the princess gave him a sword decorated with gold coins—those would come in useful!

So he flew off and bought himself a new dressing gown, and then he settled down in the woods to make up a fairy tale for the king and queen. It had to be finished by Saturday, and that's not as easy as it seems.

But at last the story was done, and Saturday had come.

The king and the queen and the whole court were at the princess's for tea; and the merchant's son was most gracefully received.

"Now you must tell us a story," said the queen. "One that is both profound and instructive."

"And funny," said the king.

"I'll try," said the merchant's son.

This is the story he told. Listen to it carefully.

Once upon a time there was a bundle of matches, who were very proud because they came of such noble stock. Their family tree—of which each of them was but a chip—had been a huge old fir tree in the forest. So now, as they lay on a shelf between a tinderbox and an old iron pot, they reminisced about their glory days.

"Yes," they said, "those were the days. We were at the very top of the tree! Diamond-tea—that is to say, dew—every morning and evening, nonstop sunshine from dawn to dusk, when the sun was shining, and all the little birds eager to tell us their stories. We were so rich we could afford to wear our best green clothes all year round; other trees spent the winter in rags and tatters. But at last the revolution came—that is to say, the woodcutter—and we were laid low. The family was split up. The trunk got a job as a mainmast on a schooner that can sail right round the world if it wants to; the branches had business here and there; and we were entrusted with the task of spreading light among the common people—that's what gentlefolk like us are doing down here in the kitchen."

"It's not been like that for me," said the iron pot which was next to the matches on the shelf. "From the moment I came into the world I've been scrubbed and put on to boil—I've lost count of the times! My job's the foundation of the home—so I'm the most important one in it. My only respite is to sit on the shelf after I've been scoured clean and enjoy a little after-dinner conversation with my friends. But apart from the bucket, which does get out to the well every so often, we're all real stay-at-homes. Of course the shopping basket does bring us all the gossip, but she's a regular firebrand, always jabbering on about the government and the people. Why, the other day her wild talk gave one old jug an apoplectic fit, and he fell down and broke into pieces."

"You do rattle on," said the tinderbox. "Can't we just enjoy ourselves?" And he

struck his steel against his flints so that the sparks flew.

"Yes," said the matches. "Let's discuss which of us is the most distinguished."

"No, I don't like to talk about myself," said an earthenware bowl. "Let's tell each other stories. I will begin with a story of everyday life; something we can all relate to."

And the bowl began, "On the shores of the Baltic, where the Danish beech trees grow . . ."

"What a beautiful beginning!" exclaimed the plates. "We're going to enjoy this!"

"There I spent my youth," continued the bowl, "in a quiet household where the furniture was always polished, the floors always scrubbed, and we had clean curtains every fortnight."

"How interestingly you put it," said the feather duster. "Your story has a woman's touch, there's something so pure and refined about it."

"I feel that too!" said the water bucket, and she gave a little jump of pleasure, so that some of her water splashed onto the floor.

Then the earthenware bowl carried on with her story—and the middle and the end were just as exciting as the beginning.

The plates all rattled with joy, and the feather duster took some parsley and crowned the bowl with a garland. She knew that would make the others jealous, but she thought, If I crown her today, she'll crown me tomorrow.

"I feel like dancing," said the fire tongs—and what a dance! When she kicked one leg up high, the old chair cushion split his seams. "Don't I get a crown?" wheedled the tongs; and she did.

Vulgar riff-raff, *thought the matches.*

Then someone called for a song from the tea urn; but the urn said it had caught a cold and could only sing if it was brought to the boil. But it was just giving itself airs; it never would sing unless it was at the table with the master and mistress.

Over on the windowsill was an old quill pen that the maid used. There was nothing remarkable about her except that she'd been dipped too far into the inkwell, which made her rather stuck-up. "If the tea urn doesn't want to sing, she needn't," said the the pen. "There's a nightingale in a cage outside; it can sing. Of course its voice is untrained, but we won't hold that against it this evening."

"I don't think it's right," said the tea kettle, which was a singer itself, and half sister to the urn, "for us to listen to a foreign bird. Is it patriotic? I think the shopping basket should decide.

"This makes me sick," said the shopping basket. "Sick to my stomach. What goings on! Isn't it about time we reformed the whole house and established a new order? That really would be something! I'll take full responsibility."

"That's it, let's have a riot!" they all shouted—but just at that moment the door opened. It was the maid. They all stood still; no one made a sound. But there wasn't one of them who wasn't thinking, I really am superior to the others; if it had been left to me, this evening would have gone with a swing.

Then the maid took the matches and lit the fire with them. My goodness, how they sputtered and blazed! Now everyone can see that we are the best, *they thought.* How bright we are! How brilliant!

And then they burned out.

"That was lovely!" said the queen. "I really felt I was right there in the kitchen with the matches. You must certainly marry our daughter."

"Absolutely," said the king. "Let's fix the wedding for Monday." Already they regarded the young man as one of the family.

On the evening before the wedding, the whole town was illuminated. Cakes and buns were distributed to the crowd; and all the little boys shouted "Hurrah!" and whistled through their fingers. It was great.

I suppose I'd better do my bit, thought the merchant's son. So he bought some rockets and whizzbangs and every sort of firework he could lay his hands on, and flew up into the air with them.

Whoosh! They went off with a bang! Such a glorious spectacle had never been seen before. The crowd nearly jumped out of their skins, and they did jump out of their slippers. Now they were sure it really was a god who was going to marry the princess.

As soon as the trunk came to earth, the merchant's son left it in the woods and returned to town to hear what people were saying about his performance—and that was only natural.

Everybody was talking about it. They all had their own views, and they were all fired up about it.

"I saw the god himself," said one. "He had eyes like sparkling stars, and a beard like a foaming torrent."

"He wrapped himself in a cloak of fire," said another, "with cherubs nestling in the folds."

What wonderful things he heard—and the next day would be his wedding day.

Now he went back to the woods to climb back into his trunk—but where was it? A spark from the fireworks had set it on fire, and the trunk was burned to ash. So the merchant's son could never fly again, and he had no way of getting to the princess.

She waited for him on the roof all day, and she is waiting still.

As for him, he goes around the world telling stories—but they are not so lighthearted as the one he told about the matches.

THE SWEETHEARTS

A whipping top and a ball were lying in a drawer along with some other toys. The top said to the ball, "Shouldn't we be sweethearts? After all, we are lying right next to each other in the drawer." But the ball, who was made of morocco leather, thought herself too much of a lady even to notice such a comment.

Next day, the little boy whose toys they were came and painted the top red and yellow and hammered a brass nail into its middle, so the top looked really splendid when he spun around.

"Look at me!" he said to the ball. "What do you say now? Shouldn't we be sweethearts? We'd be so good together—you leaping, and me dancing. No one would be happier than us."

"That's your opinion," said the ball. "You don't seem to realize that my mother and father were a pair of morocco slippers, and that I have a cork inside me."

"Yes," said the top, "but I am made of mahogany. The mayor himself turned me on his own lathe, and he was very pleased with me."

"Oh yes?" said the ball. "And I'm supposed to believe that?'

"May I never be whipped again, if I spoke a word of a lie," said the top.

"You speak very well for yourself," replied the ball, "but I can't accept you—for I am as good as half engaged to a swallow. Every time I go up in the air, he pops his head out of his nest, and says, "Will you? Will you?" and I have made up my mind to say yes—and that's as good as half engaged. But I do promise that I shall never forget you."

"That's a big help," said the top, and after that they had nothing more to say.

The next day the ball was taken out. The top watched as she flew up in the air like a bird, until she was out of sight. Every time she came back down, and when she hit the ground she bounced up high again—which was either because she wanted to, or because she had a cork inside her.

The ninth time the ball went up, she didn't come down again. The boy searched all over for her, but she was gone.

"I know where she is," sighed the top. "She's in the swallow's nest. She's going to marry the swallow."

The more the top brooded on this, the more he longed for the ball. Because he couldn't have her, he loved her more than ever. How could she choose another? It was a real puzzle. The top spun and whirled around, and all the time he was thinking about the ball. In his imagination she grew prettier and prettier. The years went by, and she became his lost love.

The top wasn't young anymore—but then one day he was painted all over with gold. He was better than new; for now he was a golden top. He whizzed around and sprang into the air for joy. That was something! But then he jumped too high and was gone.

They looked for him high and low, but they couldn't find him.

Where on earth was he?

He had jumped into the garbage can, where there was all kinds of rubbish—cabbage stalks, floor sweepings, and the contents of the gutters.

This is a fine mess I've landed myself in, thought the top. *My gilding won't last long in here. What a lot of riffraff*. He glared at a long cabbage stalk that was poking too near him, and at a strange round thing like a rotten apple. But it wasn't an apple, it was an old ball, that had lain for years in the sodden ooze of the gutter.

"Thank God! Someone to talk to at last!" said the ball, looking at the golden top. "I am made from morroco leather, and was sewn by a fine young lady, and I have a cork inside me—though you might not think so to look at me. I was going to marry a swallow, but I fell into the gutter, and I have been lying there for the past five years in the ooze. And you know, that's a long time for a young girl."

The top didn't reply. He thought of his old sweetheart, and the more he heard, the more he felt that this was she.

Then the maid came to throw something away. "Hey! Here's the golden top!" she shouted.

And the top was brought back into the house, where he was greeted with delight. No one spoke of the ball, and the top never mentioned his lost love again.

That's how it goes, when your sweetheart has lain five years in the gutter. You don't know her when you meet her in the garbage.

THE BELL

AT sunset, when the clouds glowed gold between the chimneys, the narrow streets of the city would be filled with a strange sound like the tolling of a church bell. People would hear it for a moment, and then the rumbling of the carts and the general hubbub would drown it out. "That's the evening bell," people said. "The sun's going down."

On the outskirts of the city, where the houses were spaced apart and had gardens and fields around them, the sunset was even lovelier, and the tolling of the bell was much louder. It seemed to come from a church in the heart of the still, fragrant forest. People would look in that direction, and feel quiet and thoughtful.

As time passed, one person would say to another, "Is there a church in the woods? The bell has such a strange, lovely sound. Why don't we go and look for it?"

The rich people drove in their carriages, and the poor people walked, and to all of them the road seemed very long. When they finally came to a clump of willows that grew on the edge of the forest, they sat down under the trees. Looking up into the branches, they thought they were right out in the wilds. A baker from town pitched a tent and began to sell cakes; soon there were two bakers, and the second one hung a bell over his tent. It was covered in tar to protect it from the weather, and it had no clapper.

When the people got back to town they said it had all been very romantic; and that was worth the effort, even without the tea party. Three of them said that they had gone right to the other side of the forest. They could still hear the bell, but now it seemed to be coming from the city. One wrote a whole poem about it. He said the bell was like a mother's endearments to her child; no melody could be sweeter than that bell's song.

At last the emperor heard about it, and he promised that whoever could find out where the sound came from should have the post of "Ringer of the World's Bell" even if it turned out not to be a bell at all.

So more and more people went looking for the bell, for they wanted the job. Only one came up with an explanation. He hadn't been much further into the wood than the rest, but he claimed that the bell sound came from a great owl in a hollow tree. It was the owl of wisdom, and it kept knocking its head against the trunk. He just wasn't sure whether the sound came from the bird's head or from the tree trunk. So he was made Ringer of the World's Bell, and every year he published an essay on the owl, without leaving anyone the wiser.

And now it was Confirmation Sunday. The priest had spoken so well and sincerely that the young people were all deeply moved. This was a big day for them, the day they became grown-ups. Their child-souls had to become adult and sensible.

It was beautifully sunny outside, and after the service the children who had been confirmed walked out of the city. From the forest came the powerful tolling of the big, unknown bell. They were filled with the desire to go and look for it—all except three. One of them was a girl who had to hurry home to try on her ballgown, for it was because of the dress and the ball that she had been confirmed that day; otherwise she wouldn't have come. Another was a poor boy who had borrowed both his suit and his shoes from the landlord's son, and had to take them back straight away. The third said he never went to strange places unless his parents were with him, and as he had always been a good boy, he was going to carry on being one even after he was confirmed. That's nothing to make fun of—but they all did.

So three of them stayed behind, but the others went on. The sun shone, the birds sang, and the young people sang, too. They walked hand in hand, for as they hadn't taken their places in the world yet, they were still children in the eyes of heaven.

Soon two of the smallest grew tired and turned back to town, and two girls sat down to make wreaths of wild flowers. When the rest arrived at the willow trees where the bakers had their tents, they said, "Well, here we are! Now we can see that there isn't really a bell. People just imagine it."

Just then, from deep in the woods, the bell rang out, pure and true. Five of the children made up their minds to carry on into the forest. It was hard going, for the trees grew so thickly, and the flowers grew so tall. Flowering convolvulus and brambles trailed in long garlands from tree to tree; the nightingale sang, and the sunbeams played. Oh, it was beautiful; but it was no place for girls, for their dresses would be torn to bits.

They came to some great boulders covered in different kinds of moss. A fresh spring was gurgling up, *glug, glug*.

"I wonder if that might be the bell," said one of the five, lying down to listen. "This needs looking into." So he stayed behind, and the others went on.

They came to a cottage made of branches and bark. A huge crab-apple tree was leaning over it, and roses were growing up it and over the roof. From one of its branches hung a little bell. Was that the bell they had heard? They all agreed it was, except for one boy who said that this bell was too small and delicate to be heard so far away, and that its tinkling tones could never touch the heart so deeply. But he was a king's son, and the others said, "His kind always has to know better than everyone else."

They let him go on alone. As he went on, his heart was more and more filled with the loneliness of the forest. He could still hear the little bell that the others were so pleased with, and even, when the wind

was in the right direction, the sound of singing from the tea party at the baker's tent. But the tolling of the great bell sounded ever louder; it reverberated like an organ, and it came from the left, where the heart is.

There was a rustling in the bushes, and there before the king's son stood a boy wearing wooden clogs and a jacket with sleeves so short that you couldn't help noticing his bony wrists. They recognized each other; it was the boy who couldn't join the others after the Confirmation service because he had to return his suit and shoes to the landlord's son. Now he had followed alone in his clogs and old clothes, so strong was the pull of the deep-tolling bell.

"Let's go on together," said the king's son. But the poor boy tugged at his sleeves and stared at his clogs. He mumbled that he was afraid he wouldn't be able to keep up. Besides, he thought that the bell should be looked for on the right, where everything great and glorious is.

"Then we shan't meet again," said the king's son, nodding to the poor boy, who disappeared into the densest part of the wood, where brambles and thorns would tear his old clothes to shreds and scratch his face, hands, and feet until they bled. The prince, too, got scratched, but his path lay in the sunshine. We'll follow him, for he was a bold lad.

"I will find the bell," he said, "if I have to go to the ends of the earth."

Hideous monkeys up in the trees bared their teeth in a grin and chattered to each other, "Shall we pelt him? Shall we pelt him? He's the son of a king."

But he kept on walking deeper and deeper into the forest. There, the most wonderful flowers grew: lilies like white stars, with blood-red stamens; tulips as blue as the sky, that sparkled in the wind; and apple trees with fruit like shining soap bubbles. How those trees must have glittered in the sun! He passed green meadows where deer roamed on the grass beneath oak and beech trees, and every crack in the tree bark was filled with grass and moss. There were also woodland glades with

peaceful lakes on which swans swam gracefully and flapped their wings. Often the king's son stopped to listen, thinking that the sound of the bell might be coming from one of these deep lakes, but no, it was from yet deeper in the wood that the tolling came.

Now it was sunset. The sky was red as fire, and the forest grew so still that the boy flung himself to his knees. He sang an evening hymn, and said, "I'll never find what I'm looking for. The sun is setting, and night is coming; soon it will be dark. But perhaps if I climb up those rocks, which are higher than the tallest trees, I may get one last glimpse of the round, red sun."

By catching hold of roots, he pulled himself up the wet rocks, past writhing snakes and toads that seemed to bark at him.

He reached the top just as the sun set. Oh, what magnificence! The sea, the boundless sea, stretched out before him, dashing its waves against the shore. Over where the sea met the sky stood the sun, like a great, shining altar. Everything fused together in the golden glow. The forest sang, the ocean sang, and his heart sang, too. All nature was a great holy cathedral. The trees and the floating clouds were the pillars; the flowers and grass were the woven altar cloth; and heaven itself was the dome.

The glory faded as the sun went down, but millions of stars were kindled, like so many diamond lamps. The king's son spread out his arms to it all: sky, ocean, forest. At that moment, from the right, came the poor boy in his outgrown jacket and wooden clogs. He had arrived almost as quickly, by going his own way.

The two boys ran to each other. They stood together, hand in hand, in the great cathedral of nature and poetry, and the sacred invisible bell tolled its joyful hallelujah above them.

THE LITTLE MATCH GIRL

IT was bitter cold and snowing hard, and it was almost dark; the last evening of the old year was drawing in. But despite the cold and dark, one poor little girl was still astray in the streets, with nothing on her head and nothing on her feet. She had slippers on when she left home, but they were her mother's and too big for her, and they dropped from her feet when she scampered across the road between two carriages. One slipper just disappeared and the other was snatched away by a little boy who wanted it as a doll's cradle.

So the little girl walked on, and her bare feet turned blue and raw with the cold. In her hand she carried a bundle of matches, and there were more in her ragged apron. No one had bought any matches the livelong day; no one had given her so much as a penny. And so she walked on, shivering and starved, poor girl.

The snowflakes fell on her long blond hair, which curled so prettily on her shoulders. But she was not thinking of her beauty, nor of the cold, for lights were winking from every window and the aroma of roast goose was in the air. It was New Year's Eve, and that was what the girl was thinking of.

She sat down in a sheltered corner and snuggled her feet under her, but it was no use. She couldn't get them warm. She didn't dare go home, for she had sold no matches and not earned so much as a penny. Her father would beat her, and anyway her home was nearly as cold as the street. It was an attic, and despite the straw and rags stuffed into the worst holes in the roof, the wind and snow still whistled through.

Her hands were numb with cold. If only she dared strike a single match, perhaps that would warm them. She took one out and struck it on the wall. Ah! The flame was bright and warm, and she held her hands to it. It burned for her with a magic light, until it seemed as if she were sitting by a great iron stove, with a lovely fire burning in it. The girl stretched out her feet to warm them too, but oh! The flame died down. The stove was gone, and the little girl was frozen and alone, with the burnt match in her hand.

She struck a second match against the wall. It flamed, and wherever its light fell the wall thinned to a veil so that the little girl could see into the room within. She saw a table spread with a snow-white cloth all set with fine china, and a piping hot roast goose stuffed with apples and plums. Best of all, the goose—with the knife and fork still in its breast—jumped down from the dish and waddled along the floor right up to the poor child. Then the match burned out, and the girl was left alone beside the cold, thick wall.

She kindled another match. Now she was sitting under a lovely Christmas tree, far bigger and more beautifully decorated than the one she had peeped at through the glass doors of a rich merchant's house last Christmas. A thousand candles were glimmering in the branches, and little painted figures such as she had seen in shop windows were looking down at her from the tree. The girl reached out her hand toward them, and the match went out. But still the Christmas candles burned higher and higher; she could see them twinkling like stars in the sky. Then one of them fell, leaving a trail of fiery light.

"Now someone is dying," said the little girl, for her grandmother, who was the only person who had been kind to her, but who was now dead, had told her that when a star falls, a soul is going to God.

She struck another match against the wall. It lit, and there, clear and bright in its glow, stood her old grandmother, as gentle and loving as ever.

"Grandmother!" shouted the little girl. "Take me with you! I know you will leave me when the match goes out. You will vanish like the warm stove, the delicious roast goose, and the beautiful big Christmas tree!" Feverishly the little girl struck all the rest of the matches in her bundle, to keep her grandmother there. The matches blazed like radiant bright sunshine. Never had Grandmother looked so beautiful and so tall. She lifted the little girl in her arms, and they flew together in glory and joy, higher and higher, beyond cold, beyond hunger, beyond fear, to God.

They found her in the early morning, sitting in the corner of the wall with rosy cheeks and a smile on her lips, frozen to death on the last night of the old year. The new year's sun rose over the little body, sitting with her bundle of matches all burned out. "She was trying to warm herself," people said. But no one knew what beautiful visions she had seen, nor how gloriously she and her grandmother were seeing in the glad new year.

THE COLLAR

THERE was once a man-about-town whose only belongings were a bootjack and a comb. But he had the smartest shirt collar you ever saw, and it is the collar that this story is about.

The collar was about old enough to start thinking of taking a wife, when by chance he met a lady's garter in the wash.

"Oh!" gasped the collar. "You're the sweetest thing I've ever seen—so slim, so delicate, so pretty. What's your name?"

"I shan't tell you," snapped the garter.

"Where do you live?" asked the collar.

But the garter, who had a shrinking nature, thought this was a rather personal question, so she didn't answer.

"You must be some kind of undergarment," said the collar. "A girdle, perhaps. I can see that you must be as useful as you are decorative, my dear."

"How dare you talk to me like that!" said the garter. "I never gave you permission to."

"Beauty like yours gives its own permission," said the collar.

"Keep away!" squealed the garter. "You're too . . . masculine."

"It's true I am a man-about-town," said the collar. "I own a bootjack and a comb." But it wasn't true—he was just boasting. It was his master who owned the bootjack and the comb.

"Don't come so near!" the garter fluttered. "I'm not used to it!"

"Hoity-toity!" said the collar.

Then he was lifted out of the wash. He was starched, hung to dry

over a chair in the sun, and laid on the ironing board, at the mercy of the hot iron.

"Madam," said the collar, "dear widow lady. You're getting me all hot. You're making a new man of me, you're smoothing out all my kinks. I feel I'm on fire. Oh! Be my wife!"

"Rag!" said the scornful iron, and she trundled back and forth over the collar, imagining she was a steam train. "Rag!"

The collar was a bit frayed at the edges, so the big scissors came along to trim the threads.

"Oh!" said the collar. "You must be a ballet dancer! Nobody could do the splits with more charm and grace."

"I know," said the scissors.

"You deserve to be a countess," said the collar. "All I can offer is a man-about-town, a bootjack, and a comb. If only I were a count!"

"The nerve!" said the scissors. "To propose to me!" And she gave him such a nasty cut that he would have to be thrown away.

There's nothing for it, I shall have to propose to the comb, thought the collar. "It's extraordinary, my dear," he said, "how you still have all your own teeth. Have you ever thought of getting married?"

"Didn't you know?" simpered the comb. "I'm engaged to the bootjack."

"Engaged!" said the collar.

Now there was no one left to propose to, which put him off the whole idea.

A long time passed, and then the collar found himself in the rag pile at the paper mill. There was quite a crowd of rags, but the fine ones kept their distance from the common ones, just like in life. They all had a lot to say, especially the collar, who was such a braggart.

"I had my pick of the girls," he said. "They just wouldn't leave me alone. I was a real man-about-town in those days—starched to the nines! My own bootjack and comb, which I never used! Those were the days! You should have seen me.

"I shall never forget my first love. She was a girdle—so delicate, so sweet, so pretty. She threw herself into a washtub for my sake.

"And then there was the widow. She really turned on the heat! But I snubbed her and it was her who got scorched.

"Then there was the ballet dancer. She had an artistic temperament; I still bear the scars to this day.

"My own comb was in love with me. I broke her heart, and all her teeth fell out.

"The stories I could tell! But I'm sorriest for the garter—I mean the girdle—who flung herself into the washtub. I've got a lot on my conscience. I deserve to be turned into blank paper."

And that is what happened. All the rags were pulped and made into blank paper, and the collar was made into this very page, with his own story printed on it. That's because he bragged so much afterwards about things that weren't true.

If we don't watch out, the same thing might happen to us. We'll end up in the rag pile, to be turned into blank paper and have our life story printed on it for the whole world to read—even the secret bits. Then we'll have to run around repeating it all, just like the collar.

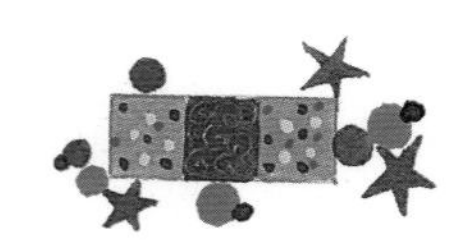

THE GOBLIN AT THE GROCER'S

THERE was once a typical student who lived in the attic and didn't own a thing, and a typical grocer who lived downstairs and owned the whole house. There was a goblin, too, and the goblin moved in with the grocer, because every Christmas Eve the grocer gave him a big lump of butter. The grocer could easily afford it, and so the goblin stayed in the shop, as you can well understand.

One evening the student came in by the back door to buy a candle and a piece of cheese; he had to run his own errands. He made his purchases and exchanged a "good evening" nod with the grocer and his wife—a woman who could do more than just nod, for she had what they call the gift of the gab. As the student nodded, his eye fell on the piece of paper wrapped round the cheese. It was a page torn from an old book, a book that ought never to have been torn up—a book of poetry.

"There's more of that book if you want it," said the grocer. "I gave an old woman some coffee beans for it. I'll let you have it for a few pennies."

"Thanks," said the student. "I'll take the book instead of the cheese. Plain bread will do me fine, and it would be a shame for the rest of the book to be torn up. You are a good man, and a practical one, but you've as much sense of poetry as that barrel!"

That was a rude thing to say—especially about the barrel—but both the grocer and the student laughed, because after all it was only said in fun. But the little goblin was annoyed that anyone should dare to speak like that to a grocer who owned the whole house and sold the best butter.

So that night, when the shop was shut and everyone but the student had gone to bed, the goblin sneaked into the bedroom and borrowed the grocer's wife's gift of the gab; she didn't need it while she was asleep. The goblin could lend the gift of the gab to anything and it would be able to speak its mind as well as you or me; but only one thing could have it at a time, which was just as well, or they'd all have spoken at once.

First the goblin lent the gift of the gab to the barrel where the grocer kept old newspapers for wrapping paper. "Is it really true," he asked, "that you have no sense of poetry?"

"Of course not," said the barrel. "I know all about it. It's the sort of thing they use to fill out the bottom of the page in a newspaper, and then people cut it out. I'm sure there's more poetry in me than in the student, and I'm only a humble barrel compared to the grocer."

Then the goblin lent the gift of the gab to the coffee mill—what a clatter!—the butter cask, and the till. They all agreed with the barrel, and the views of the majority have to be respected.

"Now for that student!" said the goblin, and he crept up the staircase to the attic where the student lived. The goblin peeked through the keyhole and saw the student reading the old book by the light of the candle.

How bright it was in there! A shaft of light was rising from the book, like a great shining tree which sheltered the student with its branches. Its leaves were a luminous green, and each flower was the head of a lovely girl—some with dark flashing eyes, and some with clear blue ones. Each fruit was a shining star which rang and sang with beautiful music.

The little goblin had never dreamed of such wonder. So he stood there on tiptoe, enraptured, until the light in the attic went out. The

student must have blown out the candle and gone to bed. But still the goblin lingered, listening as the fading echoes of the music lulled the student to sleep.

"That was amazing!" said the goblin. "I never expected that! I think I'll stay with the student." He thought it over long and hard, and then he sighed, "But the student hasn't got any butter!" So he went—yes, he went back down to the shop, and it was just as well he did, for the barrel had nearly worn out the gift of the gab, telling all the news that was inside it from one angle, and then turning round and telling it all over again from another.

The goblin took the gift of the gab back to the grocer's wife. But from then on, the whole shop, from the till to the firewood, deferred to the barrel. They held it in such high regard that in future, when the grocer read out articles from the newspaper, they thought he must have learned it all from the barrel.

But the little goblin wasn't satisfied anymore to sit and listen to the talk downstairs, however wise and well informed it was. As soon as the light glimmered down from the attic, it seemed to draw him to it by invisible cables. He just had to go and look through the keyhole.

Whenever he did, a sense of unutterable grandeur surged through him—the kind of feeling you get when God rides his storm clouds across the thundering sea. The goblin would burst into tears. He couldn't have said what he was crying for, but it comforted him. How wonderful it would be to sit with the student under that tree! But it was not to be—he had to make do with the keyhole.

He stood there on the chilly landing, but he never noticed the cold until the light went out and the music had faded away into the wind. Then he shivered! He was glad to get back to his warm corner downstairs, where he was so snug. And there was the Christmas butter to look forward to. Yes—the grocer was the one!

But in the middle of the night the goblin was woken by a terrible commotion. People in the street were banging on the shutters, and the watchman was blowing his whistle. "Fire! Fire!"

The whole street was lit up by flames. But where was the fire? Here, or next door? Everyone panicked. The grocer's wife was so flustered that she took off her gold earrings and put them in her pocket, to be sure of saving something. The grocer hunted frantically for his share certificates, and the maid ran to fetch the silk scarf she had saved up to buy. Everyone wanted to save the thing they cared about most.

The goblin was no different. He sprang up the stairs into the attic room, where the student was standing quietly looking out of the window at the fire across the road. The goblin grabbed the precious book from the table, wrapped it in his red cap, and held onto it with both hands. The house's greatest treasure was safe!

Off he ran, up to the roof and onto the highest chimney pot. And there he sat, cradling the book in his hands, while the fire over the way lit up the sky. He knew now where his heart lay, and where he really belonged.

When the fire was put out, the goblin had time to reflect.

Yes! "I'll divide my time between them," he said. "I can't forsake the grocer—because of the butter."

And that was very human! Because we, too, have to go to the grocer—for the butter.

IN A THOUSAND YEARS' TIME

Written in 1853

YES, in a thousand years' time, people will fly across the ocean on wings of steam. The young citizens of America will come to pay their respects to old Europe. They will come to see our monuments and our decaying cities, just as nowadays we tour the crumbling glories of South Asia.

In a thousand years' time, they will come.

The Thames, the Danube, and the Rhine will still be rolling on; Mont Blanc will still be wearing its cap of snow; the northern lights will still play across the northlands. Generation after generation will have come to dust. The great men of our day will be as forgotten as the Viking chieftain whose funeral mound some prosperous farmer has turned into a viewpoint where he can sit and gaze out over his waving fields of corn.

"To Europe!" cry the young Americans. "To the land of our fathers, to the wonderful land of memories and dreams—to Europe!"

Here comes the airship. It will be crowded, for it is much faster to fly than to sail. The electro-magnetic cable under the ocean has already telegraphed ahead the passenger list of this air caravan.

The coast of Ireland is reached first; but the passengers are still asleep; they are not to be woken until they arrive in England. There they will set foot in the land of Shakespeare, as the cultured ones call it; the others call it the land of Democracy, or the land of the Industrial Revolution.

The tourists will devote a whole day to England and Scotland; then their journey continues through the Channel Tunnel to France, the country of Charlemagne and Napoleon. Some of them have heard of Molière, too, but the arguments of the classical and romantic schools are all in the past; the names on the tourists' lips are of celebrities, poets, and scientists of whom our age has never heard—they have yet to be born, in that cradle of Europe, Paris.

The airship will then fly over the country from which Columbus sailed, where Cortés was born, and where Calderón composed his dramas in flowing verse. Beautiful dark-eyed women still live in its fertile valleys, and their folk songs still name El Cid and the palace of Alhambra.

Through the air once more, to Italy, where the Eternal City of Rome once stood. It has been wiped out. The Campagna is a desert; one wall of St. Peter's is still standing, but there are doubts whether it is genuine.

Then to Greece, to spend a night in the luxury hotel on Mount Olympus—just to say that they have been there. Next stop is the Bosporus, for a few hours' rest on the site of Byzantium. A handful of poor fishermen spreading their nets still remember old tales of the harems that stood here in days gone by.

Then the airship flies along the Danube, allowing glimpses of ruined cities below, cities our age never knew. Every now and then the ship will land to allow the tourists to admire some monument that belongs to their past, but our future.

Then the airship is aloft again. Below lies Germany, which was once crisscrossed by railroads and canals—Germany, the land where Luther spoke, and Goethe sang, and Mozart made his music. But when they speak of science and the arts, their talk will be of names we do not know.

One day is given to Germany, and one to the whole of Scandinavia—the homelands of Ørsted and Linnaeus, and Norway, the young country of the old heroes. Iceland is a stop on the homeward journey. The geyser no long spouts, and the volcano has died, but the rocky island still stands in the foaming sea, the memorial stone of the sagas.

"There's a lot to see in Europe," say the young Americans. "You need a whole week, as So-and-so has shown in his guidebook, *See Europe in Seven Days*."

FIVE PEAS FROM THE SAME POD

THERE were once five peas in a pod; they were green, and the pod was green, so they thought that the whole world was green, and that was quite right. The pod grew and the peas grew; they all made space for each other, five in a row. The sun shone and kept the pod warm, and the rain fell and kept it clean. It was a snug little home, light in the day and dark at night, just as it should be. As the peas grew, they began to think for themselves; after all, they had to do something to pass the time.

"Shall I be stuck here forever?" each said in turn. "I'm afraid I'll get hard from sitting here so long. I wonder if there's something outside; I have a feeling there is."

Weeks passed. The peas turned yellow and the pod turned yellow. "The whole world is turning yellow," they said, and they had a perfect right to say it.

Then they felt the pod being pulled; they were in a man's hand, being shoved into a pocket alongside some other pods. "Soon we shall be opened," they said. That's what they were waiting for.

"I wonder which of us will go farthest," said the smallest pea. "We'll soon see."

"What will be, will be," said the biggest.

Pop! The pod split, and all five peas rolled out into the bright sun. They were in a little boy's hand. He said they were just the peas for his peashooter.

He fired off the first.

"Now I'm flying out into the wide world! Catch me if you can!" and it was gone.

"I shall fly right up to the sun," said the second. "That's the pod for me!" And off it went.

"We don't care, so long as we keep rolling!" said the next two, for they were rolling on the floor. But they went into the peashooter anyway. "We'll go farthest!" they cried.

"What will be, will be," said the last pea, as it was shot into the air. It lodged in a crack in the attic windowsill; the rotten wood was already stuffed with moss and earth, and the pea stuck there. It lay hidden, though not hidden from God.

"What will be, will be," it said.

In the little attic room lived a poor woman who did heavy work, such as cleaning stoves and chopping wood. But though she was strong and willing, however hard she worked she was still as poor as ever. Living with her was her daughter, who had been lying in bed for a whole year. The little girl was terribly thin and delicate; it seemed she could neither live nor die.

"She'll go to her little sister," said the woman. "I had two children, but it was so hard to look after them both, so God went shares with me and took one for himself. I'd like to keep the other, but God doesn't want them to be parted, so she'll go to her sister."

But the sick girl stayed on. She lay patient and quiet in bed all day, while her mother went out to earn their keep.

It was spring, and one sunny morning, just as the mother was getting ready to go out to work, the girl noticed something through the lowest windowpane. "Whatever is that green thing, peeping in at the window? It's swaying in the breeze."

The mother opened the window a crack. "Well!" she said. "It's a little pea plant; you can tell by the green leaves. However did that get there? It will be a little garden for you to look at."

So the sickbed was moved nearer to the window, so the girl could keep an eye on the pea as it sprouted, while the mother was at work.

"I feel I'm getting better, Mother," said the young girl that evening. "The sun has been shining in on me so warmly today. The little pea is getting stronger, and so am I. Soon I will be out in the sunshine, too!"

"I hope so," said the mother, but she did not believe it. Still, because the little plant had given her daughter such cheer, she found a stick and tied it up, so that the wind wouldn't break it. And she ran a string up the window, to give the pea something to climb up, which it did. You could see it grow from one day to the next.

"I do believe it's going to flower," said the mother one morning, and now she too began to hope that her sick daughter might get well. She thought how lately the girl's talk had been livelier, and how each morning she sat herself up in bed and looked with sparkling eyes at her little garden of one pea plant.

Next week, the girl got up for the first time and sat happily in the sunshine for a whole hour. The window was open, and the pea's pink flower was in bloom. The girl leaned out and kissed the delicate petals. That was a red letter day.

"God himself planted that pea and made it thrive to bring hope to you and joy to me, my darling," said the happy mother, and she smiled at the flower as though it were an angel from heaven.

But what happened to the other peas? The one who flew out into the wide world shouting, "Catch me if you can!" was swallowed by a pigeon. He lay in its stomach like Jonah in the whale. The two who didn't care did no better, for they were eaten by pigeons, too, so at least they made themselves useful. But the other one—the one who wanted to fly up into the sun—that one fell down into the gutter and lay there for weeks in the dirty water. It began to bloat.

"I'm on the way up," it said. "Soon I shall be so fat I shall burst, and that's as much as any other pea can do, or ever has ever done. I'm the most remarkable of the five peas in our pod."

And the gutter agreed.

But the little girl stood at the attic window with shining eyes and glowing cheeks. She folded her delicate hands over the pea flower and gave thanks to God for it.

"I still think my pea's the best," said the gutter.

THE BEETLE

THE emperor's horse was given gold shoes—a gold shoe for each hoof.

Why was he given gold shoes?

He was a handsome beast—good legs, wise eyes, and a mane that fell over his neck like a silken veil. He had borne his master through bullets and smoke on the battlefield—he had used his teeth and hooves to clear a way through the enemy and had jumped right over a fallen horse to carry the emperor to safety. He had saved the emperor's golden crown, and his life as well—and that was even more precious than gold. So that was why he was give gold shoes—a gold shoe for each hoof.

Then the dung beetle came out of the manure heap.

"First the big, then the little," he said, holding out a foot to the blacksmith. "Not that size is important."

"What do you want?" asked the smith.

"Gold shoes," replied the beetle.

"Are you mad?" said the smith. "Why should you get gold shoes?"

"Why not?" said the beetle. "Aren't I as good as that clumsy brute, who needs to be waited on hand and foot—groomed, fed, and watered? Don't I live in the same stable?"

"But why has the horse been given its gold shoes? You don't understand!"

"Understand! I understand when I'm not wanted!" said the beetle. "Insults and ridicule! I've had enough. I'm going out into the world to make my fortune."

"Good riddance to bad rubbish," said the smith.

"Oaf!" said the beetle.

Then the beetle flew outside, to a flower garden filled with the scent of roses and lavender.

"Isn't it lovely here?" asked a ladybug, showing off the smart black spots on her red wings. "Isn't it fragrant?"

"It's not a patch on what I'm used to," said the beetle. "Call this beautiful? Why, there isn't even a manure heap."

The beetle flew over to the shade of a gillyflower, on which a furry caterpillar was crawling. "What a wonderful world this is!" said the caterpillar. "The sun is so warm; everything is perfect. And when I fall asleep—what some people call dying—I shall wake up as a butterfly."

"Wherever did you get such a notion?" said the beetle. "Don't give yourself airs! I come from the emperor's stable, and no one there—not even the emperor's horse—has ideas like that. Go on, grow some wings and fly away! I'm going to." And the beetle flew off.

"I try not to get annoyed," he muttered, "but I am annoyed, all the same." So he dropped onto the lawn, and went to sleep.

Then the heavens opened—it poured with rain. The beetle was woken up by the rain, and he tried to burrow into the earth, but he couldn't. The water overturned him—now he was swimming on his front, now his back. Flying was out of the question. It looked like this would be the end for him. There was nothing to do but lie there—so there he lay.

When the rain stopped for a moment and the beetle blinked the water out of his eyes, he caught sight of something white. It was a piece of linen left out on the grass to dry. It was soaking wet. The beetle crept into a fold. It wasn't as good as the manure heap, but beggars can't be choosers. So he stayed there for a day and a night, and the rain stayed too. The beetle didn't poke his head out of the fold until morning; he was that vexed.

Two frogs came and plopped down on the linen. Their eyes were shining with pleasure. "What glorious weather!" one said. "It's so refreshing, and this linen really soaks it up! You could swim in it!"

The other said, "I'd like to know if the swallow, who can't stay in one place for five minutes, has ever come across a better climate than ours. Such drizzle and damp! It's as good as living in a ditch. A frog who is tired of such weather is tired of life."

"I don't suppose you've ever been in the emperor's stables," said the beetle, "but there, the wetness is spicy and warm. That's my kind of damp—but you can't take it with you when you travel. Can you tell me, is there a greenhouse in this garden, where a refined type like me would feel at home?"

The frogs couldn't understand him—or rather they wouldn't.

"I only ask once," said the beetle, after he had asked three times and never got an answer.

He went on and came to a bit of broken flowerpot. It shouldn't have been left lying there; but as it had been, several families of earwigs had taken shelter under it. Earwigs don't need a lot of room; but they do like company. The mothers all love their children and think that they are the cleverest and most beautiful of all.

"My boy is engaged already," said one. "The little innocent! So full of boyish pranks! His ambition is to climb into a priest's ear. Bless him!"

"My boy," said another, "is a likely lad—he came sizzling out of the egg, and he's sowing his wild oats already. And that warms a mother's heart. Don't you agree, Mr. Beetle?" For she had recognized him by his shape.

"You are both right," said the beetle, so they invited him to come in and make himself at home.'

"You must meet my little one," said a third mother.

"They're such sweethearts, and so full of fun," said a fourth. "They're never naughty unless they have a tummy ache—though they do get rather a lot of those."

All the mothers chattered on about their children, and the children themselves pulled at the beetle's beard with the little pincers they have in their tail.

"The little rascals!" said the mothers. "Always up to something!" And they positively dribbled with motherly love. But the beetle was bored, and asked directions to the greenhouse.

"It's far, far away, on the other side of the ditch," said one of the earwig mothers. "If one of my children were to travel so far from home, it would be the death of me."

"All the same that's where I'm going," said the beetle, and he left without saying goodbye, as important people do.

In the ditch he came across some relatives—all dung beetles.

"We live here," they said. "We're as snug as bugs. It's the land of plenty! Come in; you must have had a tiring journey."

"Yes, I have," said the beetle. "I've been lying on linen in the rain, and there's only so much cleanliness a beetle can bear. And now I've got aches and pains in my wings from standing under a drafty piece of flowerpot. What a relief to be back among my own kind!"

"Do you come from the greenhouse?" asked the oldest of them.

"Higher up," said the beetle. "I was born with gold shoes on my feet; I come from the emperor's stable. Now I've been sent on a secret mission. But it's no use pumping me about it—I won't say a word."

With that the beetle eased itself down into the mud.

There were three girl beetles there, giggling out of nervousness.

"They're none of them engaged," said their mother, and the girls giggled out of shyness.

"Even in the royal stables, I've never seen more beautiful girls," said the adventurous beetle.

"Don't take advantage of my little girls! Don't pay court to them unless you mean it. But I see you are a gentleman, so I give you my blessing."

"Hurrah!" cried all the others, and so the beetle became engaged. First engaged; then married; there was no reason for delay.

The first day was good enough; the second jogged along; but by the third day it was all too much—he couldn't be doing with wives and maybe even children.

They took me by surprise, thought the beetle. *So now I'll surprise them.*

And he did. He ran away. His wives waited all day and all night, and then they knew they had been abandoned. The other beetles said, "He was a good-for-nothing playboy," because now they would have to take care of his deserted wives.

"So now you are innocent young girls again," said their mother. "But shame on that no-good for leaving you like that!"

In the meantime the beetle was sailing across the ditch on a cabbage leaf. Two men taking a morning stroll happened to see him, and picked him up. They turned him this way and that and looked at him from every angle, for they were experts.

The younger one said, "'Allah sees the black beetle in the black stone in the black mountain.' Isn't that what it says in the Koran?" And then he translated the beetle's name into Latin and gave an account of its species and their habits. But the older one said, "There's no need to take this one home; we have better specimens already."

The beetle's feelings were hurt by this, so he flew out of the scholar's hand and up into the sky. His wings had dried off, so he made it all the way to the greenhouse. A window was open, so he flew straight in and make himself at home in some fresh manure.

"This is the life!" he said.

Soon he fell asleep and dreamed that the emperor's horse was dead and that he, Mr. Beetle, had been given its gold shoes and promised two more. It was a sweet dream.

When the beetle woke up, he climbed out of the manure and took a look about him. How magnificent the greenhouse was! The sun was shining down through the palm leaves onto flowers as red as fire, as

yellow as amber, and as white as new-fallen snow.

"Such greenery!" exclaimed the beetle. "It will be delicious once it goes bad. What a fine larder! Now I must see if I can find any of my relations here. I can't mix with just anybody; I have my pride and I'm proud of it." And then he allowed himself to daydream about the emperor's horse dying, and being given its gold shoes.

Suddenly a hand grabbed the beetle, pinching him and turning him over.

It was the gardener's son and one his friends; they had seen the beetle and wanted to have some fun with him. They wrapped him in a vine leaf and put him in a warm trouser pocket, where he wriggled about until he got another pinch from the gardener's son.

The boys ran down to the lake at the bottom of the garden. They made a boat out of an old wooden clog. A stick was the mast, and the beetle—who was tied to the stick with a thread of wool—was the captain. Then the boat was launched.

The lake was so big the beetle thought it was the ocean. He flipped over on his back from fright and lay there lashed to the mast, with all his legs kicking in the air.

The wooden clog sailed across the water. When it got too far out, one of the boys would roll up his trousers and fetch it back. But then, the boys were wanted. They were called so sharply they ran home and forgot all about the boat. It drifted on and on. The beetle was terrified, but he couldn't fly away, as he was tied to the mast.

A fly buzzed up to him.

"Lovely weather we're having," said the fly. "And what a delightful spot this is. Just the place for a snooze in the sun."

"Stuff and nonsense!" said the beetle. "Can't you see I'm tied up?"

"I'm not tied up," said the fly, and flew away.

"Now I know the world," said the beetle. "It's a mean world, and I'm the only decent one in it. First I'm refused my gold shoes; then I'm made to lie on damp linen and stand in a draft; then I'm tricked into marriage. When I boldly set out into the world to try my luck, up comes some human puppy who ties me up and sets me adrift on the raging waves. And all this while the emperor's horse is prancing around in his gold shoes! That's what really riles me. And do I get any sympathy?

"What a life I've had—but what's the use if no one knows my story? The world doesn't deserve to hear it. Not after refusing me gold shoes when the emperor's horse just had to stretch out its legs for them. No, they had their chance. I would have been a credit to the stable. But it's their loss; the world's loss. It's all over."

But all was not over, for two girls were rowing on the pond.

"Look! There's a wooden clog!" said one.

"It's got a beetle tied up in it!" said the other. And she lifted the boat out of the water and carefully cut the thread with a small pair of scissors, without harming the beetle. When they reached the shore, she set him down safely on the grass. "Off you go!" she said. "Crawl small or fly high—go on, try!"

The beetle flew straight in through the open window of a large building—and collapsed into the long silken mane of the emperor's horse, who was standing in the stable where they both belonged. He clung tight to the mane while he tried to gather his thoughts.

Here I am, sitting on the emperor's horse, riding high. . . . What was that? Yes, now it's coming clear. Now I understand. Why was the horse given gold shoes? That's what the smith asked me. And now I know. It's for me. That's why the horse was given gold shoes.

The beetle was happy now. "Travel broadens the mind," he said, "and puts everything into perspective."

The sun shone bright through the window. "It's not such a bad world after all," said the beetle, "if you learn to roll with the punches." All was right with the world now, for the emperor's horse had been given gold shoes so that the dung beetle could ride him.

Now I'll dismount, thought the beetle, *and go and tell the other beetles what*

has been done for me. I'll tell them all my adventures in the wide world. But I won't go on my travels again. I'll stay at home, until the horse wears out his gold shoes.

THE TOAD

THE well was deep, so the bucket was on a long rope, and water was hard to fetch. Although the water was clear, the sun never reached down far enough to touch it; but as far as it did shine, green moss grew between the stones.

A family of toads lived there. They were newcomers; they had followed their mother when she fell head over heels down the well. The green frogs, who had lived there swimming in the water for ages, called them "cousins," and pretended the toads were only on a visit. But the toads had no intention of leaving. They liked it in the "dry part" of the well, as they called the damp stones.

Mother frog had once been on a journey—all the way to the top in the water bucket. But the light hurt her eyes. Luckily she managed to scramble out of the bucket and fall back *splosh!* into the well—where she lay for three whole days with a bad back. She hadn't much to tell about the world above—only that the well was not the whole world. Mother toad could have told them more than that, but she never answered when she was spoken to, and so they never asked her.

"She's fat, ugly, and slimy," said the children, "and her brats are slimier still."

"That's as may be," said mother toad, "but one of them has a precious jewel in their head—or is that me?"

The young frogs didn't like the sound of that; they pulled faces at her and dived back into the water. But the young toads stretched their hind legs in sheer pride, and held their heads perfectly still.

Then they pestered their mother. "What is it we're being proud of?"

they asked. "What is a jewel?"

"It is something so valuable and fine," said mother toad, "that I can't begin to describe it. You wear it for your own pleasure, and to upset other people. And that's enough of your questions; I've said my say."

"Well I'm sure I don't have the jewel," said the littlest toad. "It sounds too precious for the likes of me. And if it would upset other people, it wouldn't give me pleasure. All I wish is that I could go to the top of the well, just once, and look out. That must be wonderful."

"Best stay put," said mother toad. "You know where you are here, and here's where you belong. Stay out of the way of that bucket, or it might squash you; and if you do get caught in it, jump out. Though there's no guarantee you'll land as well as I did, with legs and eggs intact."

Croak! said the littlest toad, as if she were swallowing her words.

But she still longed to go to the top of the well and glimpse the green world above; so next morning when the water bucket was lowered, the little toad, quivering with excitement, jumped off its ledge into the full bucket, and was hauled to the top.

"*Ugh!* What an ugly brute!" said the man who had pulled it up—and he poured the water away and aimed a kick at the toad. She only just escaped being badly hurt by hopping into some nettles.

In among the nettles, the toad looked up and saw the sun shining through the leaves, which seemed transparent; it was the same as when we go into a tall wood and look up to the sun filtering through the high branches.

"It's much nicer here than in the well," said the little toad. "I could stay here forever." She stayed for one hour; she stayed for two. But then she began to wonder what lay beyond the nettle patch. "As I've come this far, I might as well go on."

She hopped out onto a road. The sun was hot on her back, and she was soon coated with dust from the highway. "This really *is* dry land," she said. "It's almost too much of a good thing; it's making me itch."

She came to the ditch, where forget-me-nots and meadowsweet grew; in the hedge were elder and hawthorn, twined round with flowering bindweed. What a picture it was! And there was a butterfly fluttering about, which the toad decided must be a flower that had left home to see the world—and that was quite a shrewd guess.

"If only I could go so fast," said the toad. *Croak! Croak!* "It's so nice here."

She stayed in the ditch for eight days and nights, and never went short of food. But on the ninth day she thought, *I must be getting along.* Though it was hard to imagine that anywhere could be more delightful than the ditch, yet it was lonely; and the wind last night had carried the sounds of other toads or frogs.

"It's wonderful to be alive," she said, as she set off once more. "It's wonderful to come up out of the well, to lie in a forest of nettles, to march across a dusty road, and to rest in a wet ditch; but I must go on. I'll look for those other toads or frogs, for one can't do without company. Nature is not enough!"

She made her way through the hedge into a field and across it to a pond surrounded by reeds.

"Isn't this a bit wet for you?" said the frogs who lived there. "But you're welcome all the same—a girl just as much as a boy."

They invited the toad to join them for a singsong that evening. A lot of bellowing in squeaky voices—you know the kind of thing. There were no refreshments, just all the water you could drink.

"I must be getting on," said the little toad. She felt a desire for something better.

She saw the stars twinkling in the sky; she saw the new moon; she saw the sun rising ever higher. *I am still in a well*, she thought. *But a bigger well. I must go higher yet. I'm so restless; I feel strange longings in me.*

Later, when the moon was full, the poor creature thought, *I wonder if that is the bucket being lowered down for me to jump into. That would take me higher! Or maybe the sun is the great bucket—it shines so brightly, and I'm sure it's big enough to take us all. I must take my chance when it comes. Oh! how my head is filled with its light. I'm sure it gleams brighter than any jewel. So I don't regret not having one of those. I just want to go higher; higher to glory and joy. I have faith, and yet I'm fearful. The first step is so hard; but I must go on—onward and upward!*

And she put her best foot forward, and soon came back to the road. Then she came to a place where humans lived—there were both flower and vegetable gardens, and the toad rested under a cabbage leaf.

"How many different creatures there are!" she said. "There's always something new in this big, lovely world! As long as you keep on the move!" She took a look around the vegetable garden. "How green it is!"

"I should say it is," said a caterpillar that was sitting on a cabbage leaf. "And my leaf is the greenest of them all. It's so big it covers half the world; but that's the half I don't bother myself about."

Cluck! Cluck! The hens were coming. The one at the front had the sharpest eyesight—she spied the caterpillar on the leaf and pecked at it. It fell to the ground and lay there wriggling. The hen peered at it first with one eye and then with the other, wondering what all that wriggling was for. *It can't be doing it for fun*, she thought; and she lifted her head to strike.

The toad was horrified, and began to crawl at the hen.

It's called up reinforcements, thought the hen. *A horrible crawling thing! It would only have tickled my throat, anyway*. So she left the caterpillar alone.

"I wriggled out of that one," said the caterpillar. "I kept my nerve. But the problem is, how do I get back onto my cabbage leaf? Where is it?"

The little toad offered her sympathy to the caterpillar and said she was glad her ugliness had frightened the hen away.

"What do you mean?" said the caterpillar. "I saved myself by my own

wriggling. Though it's true you are ugly. I don't owe you a thing. Now where's my leaf? I smell cabbage. . . . Here it is! There's no place like home. But I must climb up higher."

Yes, higher! thought the little toad. *Ever higher! It feels just as I do. A fright like that would give anyone a funny turn. But we all want to go higher.*

The little toad looked up as high as it could. On the farmhouse roof was a stork's nest, and father stork and mother stork were chatting away with their long beaks. *Imagine living so high up*, thought the toad. *If only I could go up there!*

Inside the farmhouse lived two students. One was a poet, and the other was a naturalist. The first sang and wrote about the wonder of God's creation, and how it was mirrored in his heart. His poems were short and simple yet full of meaning. The second looked at the world itself, in all its individual parts. He considered the creation as a matter of science—add here, take away there, and eventually the sum works out. He wanted to know and understand it all. He had a searching mind; a fine mind. They both loved life.

"Look, there's a good specimen of a toad," said the naturalist. "I'll catch it and preserve it in alcohol."

"You've already got two. Leave it in peace," said the poet.

"But it's so wonderfully ugly," said the naturalist.

"If only we could find the precious jewel in its head, it might be worth dissecting it," said the poet.

"Precious jewel!" said the other. "What kind of natural history is that?"

"It's folklore, not natural history. I like the thought that the toad, the ugliest of creatures, has a precious jewel hidden inside its head. It's the same way with human beings—think of the precious jewels that Aesop and Socrates had inside their ugly mugs."

The two friends walked away, and the toad escaped being preserved in alcohol. So she didn't hear any more and didn't understand half of what she had heard. But she knew they had been talking about the precious jewel. *It's just as well I don't have it, or I might have been in trouble*, she thought.

Father stork was still chattering away on the roof. He was giving his family a lecture, and keeping an eye on the young men in the garden at the same time. "Human beings are the most conceited of all animals," he said. "Listen to them jabbering away in their silly lingo. They're so proud of being able to speak, yet if they travel as far as we storks go in a single day, they find they can't understand a word! Whereas we storks speak the same tongue all over the world—the same in Egypt as in Denmark.

"And humans can't fly at all! They have to get in a machine that does it for them, and then they break their silly necks in it! It gives me shivers up and down my beak to think of it. The world can do without them. We don't need them; all we need are frogs and worms."

What a magnificent speech, thought the little toad. *The stork must be a very important creature, it lives so high up. I've never seen anything like it.* Just then the stork launched itself into the air. *And it can swim too!* thought the toad.

Meanwhile mother stork was telling her children all about Egypt, and the waters of the river Nile, and all the glorious mud to be found in foreign parts. It all sounded wonderful to the toad.

"I must go to Egypt," she said. "If only the stork will take me with him—or perhaps one of the youngsters would. I'd pay him back somehow. Yes, I'll go to Egypt, I'm sure of it. I'm so lucky. I'm sure my dreams are better than any precious jewel."

But she *did* have the most precious jewel—her endless longing to go upward, ever upward. That was the jewel, and it gleamed with joy and yearning.

At that moment the stork came. He had seen the toad in the grass. He snatched her up in his beak, squeezing her in half. It hurt, but the little toad was sure she was going to Egypt. Her eyes shone with anticipation—it was as though a spark was flying out of them.

Croak!

Her heart gave up; the toad was dead.

But what of the spark that flew from her eyes? What of that?

The spark was caught up in a sunbeam and carried away. But where was it taken, that precious jewel from inside the toad's ugly head?

Don't ask the naturalist; ask the poet. He'll tell you the answer in a fairy tale. A caterpillar will be in the story; and a family of storks, too. The caterpillar transforms itself into a butterfly; the stork flies right across the ocean to Africa, then finds the shortest way home again to Denmark—back to the very same nest. It's almost too magical and mysterious—yet it's true. Go and ask the naturalist—he'll have to admit it. And you know it yourself, for you have seen it with your own eyes.

But what about the jewel in the toad's head?

Seek it in the sun! You might find it there!

But the light is too bright. We do not have eyes that can gaze on all the glory that God has created. But we shall get them one day. That will be the most wonderful fairy tale of all; for we shall be in it ourselves.

DANCE, DANCE, DOLLY MINE!

"THAT must be a song for very little children," declared Aunt Malle. "I think it's silly, that 'Dance, dance, dolly mine!'"

But little Amalie liked it—she was only three years old, and she was always playing with her dolls. She was bringing them up to be as clever as Aunt Malle.

There was a student who came to the house to help Amalie's brothers with their homework, and he often took the time to talk to Amalie and her dolls. He wasn't like anyone else—Amalie thought he was very funny. Aunt Malle said he had no idea how to speak to children—their little heads couldn't possibly take in his tomfoolery. But little Amalie's could—she even learned by heart all the words of his ditty, "Dance, dance, dolly mine!" and sang it to her three dolls. Two of them were new—a girl and a boy—but the third was old. Her name was Lisa, and she liked listening to the song because she was mentioned in it.

Dance, dance, dolly mine!
Oh, you look so very fine!
And your boyfriend looks good too,
In trousers of white and jacket of blue—
He wears his hat and gloves just so,
And shoes so tight they pinch his toe.
He is fine and she is fine,
Dance, dance, dolly mine!

DANCE, DANCE, DOLLY MINE!

Look, look, Lisa's here,
My dear dolly from last year!
She has brand-new flaxen hair
And a face that's clean and fair.
She really looks quite young again—
Come to me, my old friend.
You must join the fun, and so
The three of you—put on a show.

Dance, dance, my dollies bright,
Get the steps and rhythm right.
Keep your back straight, don't forget,
Point your toe and pirouette.
The dance is nearly over now—
Leap, twirl, and take a bow.
You really are a sight to see—
Dance, dance, my dollies three.

The dolls understood the song, little Amalie understood it, and the student understood it too—but then, he had written it, and he said it was an excellent song. Only Aunt Malle did not understand it—she had long since climbed over the fence between childhood and adulthood, so she thought it was nonsense. But little Amalie didn't agree, and she kept on singing the song.

It is from her singing that we have it.

THE GARDENER AND HIS MASTER

A FEW miles from the capital stood an old manor house with thick walls, towers, and stepped gables. It was the summer home of a rich nobleman and his wife; it was the best and handsomest of all the houses they owned. It was so well kept it looked as if it was new built, and inside it was comfortable and welcoming. The family arms were carved in stone over the entrance, surrounded by climbing roses.

The garden in front of the house was laid to lawn, with both pink and white may trees. There were even rare flowers of the kind you usually see in a greenhouse, for the nobleman employed a skilled gardener. The flower garden, the orchard, even the kitchen garden were delightful. By the kitchen garden you could still make out some of the original garden design, with box hedges clipped into the shape of crowns and pyramids. Beyond that towered two ancient trees, almost bare of leaves, that looked as if the wind had been pelting them with great lumps of muck—but every lump was a bird's nest.

Here, for time out of mind, rooks and crows had built their nests. The two old trees were a regular settlement of screaming birds. They were the oldest family on the estate, and they regarded themselves as its true masters. They scorned the flightless creatures below, and didn't pay them much attention except when they started banging away with their guns, when the birds would flap into the air squawking *Caw! Caw!*

The gardener often suggested cutting the trees down, as they were an eyesore, and if they were gone, the screaming birds would go, too. But the master wouldn't hear of it, for the trees and the birds were part of the garden—something from the old days, that shouldn't just be thrown away.

"Those trees belong to the birds now. Leave them alone, my good Larsen," he would say. The gardener's name was Larsen, though that's neither here nor there. "Haven't you got enough to do already, Larsen, what with the flower garden, the orchard, the kitchen garden, and the greenhouse?"

It was true, the gardener was responsible for all these, and he worked hard and well. The master and mistress knew this, but all the same they couldn't resist telling him every now and then how they had seen flowers or eaten fruit at other people's houses that were better than anything in their garden. The gardener was always cast down at this, for he did his best. He had a good heart, and he was good at his job.

One day the master sent for him and told him—in a friendly but patronizing way—that the day before, while dining with some distinguished friends, they had been served apples and pears so juicy and mouthwatering that all the guests had been really impressed. The fruit was obviously not homegrown, but if it would stand the climate, it should be imported. As the fruit was known to have been bought at the city's leading greengrocer's, the gardener should ride in and find out where the apples and pears were from, and order cuttings.

The gardener knew the greengrocer's well, for that was where, with his master's permission, he sold off the surplus fruit and vegetables from the garden. So he went to town and asked the greengrocer where he had got the apples and pears that had been so admired.

"Why, they were from your own garden!" said the greengrocer. He showed the gardener some of the fruit, and he recognized it at once.

The gardener was thrilled. He hurried home and told his master the good news that the fruit came from his own garden.

But the master and mistress wouldn't believe it. "There must be some mistake, Larsen. Go and get the greengrocer to put it in writing."

So Larsen got a written certificate from the greengrocer.

"How strange!" said the master.

From then on, the dining table at the manor always had a great bowl filled with apples and pears from the garden. The master had fruit crated up and sent as presents to friends in the city and elsewhere—some even overseas. What an excitement! Though they had to admit that it had been an unusually good year for fruit trees across the country.

Some time later the master and mistress were invited to dine with the king. The next day, they sent for the gardener. The king had served some exquisite melons from the royal greenhouse.

"You must go to the royal gardener, Larsen, and ask him for some melon seeds."

"But the royal gardener got his seeds from us," said Larsen, highly delighted.

"Then the man has improved the fruit in some way," snapped the master. "Every melon was perfect."

"I'm very pleased to hear it," said Larsen. "I should explain that the royal gardener has had no luck with his melons this year. When he saw ours, he begged three of them for the king's table."

"Do you mean to say that we were eating our own melons?"

"I'm sure you were." And Larsen went to the royal gardener and got him to write a certificate confirming that the king's melons had come from the manor garden.

The master was quite taken aback. But soon he was showing the certificate around, and sending melon seeds far and wide, just as he had with the apples and pears.

The seeds were a great success, and they were named after the manor house—so now the house's name was known in England, Germany, and France. Who would have thought it?

"I do hope the gardener won't let it go to his head," said the master.

He didn't; but he did want to become one of the best gardeners in the land. Each year he tried to excel at something, and he often succeeded. But people often said that nothing was ever quite as good as his very first fruit, the apples and pears. The melons, of course, were good in their way; his strawberries were all very well, but no bigger or juicier than those to be found elsewhere.

The year the radishes failed, no one could talk of anything else, although other things had turned out well. It was almost as if the master felt quite relieved to be able to say, "A poor year, Larsen." It pleased him to say it: "A poor year."

Twice a week the gardener would take fresh flowers up to the house. He arranged them with great skill, so that nothing clashed; each bouquet was a delight.

"You're blessed with good taste, Larsen," said the mistress. "Though of course that's a gift from God, and nothing to be proud of."

One day his arrangement was a crystal bowl with a water lily leaf floating on the surface. On top of this, with its stalk going down into the water, was a brilliant blue flower as big as a sunflower.

"An Indian lotus flower!" exclaimed the mistress. She had never seen anything like it.

The bowl was placed where the sun would catch it in the daytime, and it would reflect the candlelight at night. Everyone who saw it thought it was as lovely as it was unusual.

The young princess—who was good and kind—admired it so much that the master and mistress gave it to her to take back to the royal castle. Then they went into the garden to try to pick another for themselves; but they couldn't find one. So they called the gardener and asked him where he had got the Indian lotus flower from. "We've looked everywhere," they said. "It's not in the greenhouse or in the flower garden."

"No, it's not," said the gardener. "It is only a humble flower from the kitchen garden. But all the same, it's lovely isn't it? It's like a blue cactus, the flower of the artichoke."

"You should have made that perfectly clear," said the master, "instead of letting us think it was a rare foreign flower. Now you've shown us up in front of the princess. She was so taken with the flower that we gave it to her. She knows a lot about botany, and she didn't know what it was; but then, botany doesn't have anything to do with vegetables. My good Larsen, how could you have sent such a thing into the house? You've made fools of us."

So the beautiful blue flower from the kitchen garden was banished from the manor house, where it didn't belong. The master sent his apologies to the princess, explaining that the lotus flower was nothing but a common vegetable. It was the gardener's fault, and he had been given a good dressing down for his impudence.

"What a shame! It's not fair," said the princess. "He has opened our eyes to a beautiful flower that we had overlooked. I will order the royal gardener to bring me an artichoke flower every day, for as long as they are in bloom."

And she did; so the master and mistress told Larsen that, after all, he might bring them another artichoke blossom. "It really is a remarkable flower," they said, and they complimented Larsen on it.

"Larsen loves praise," they said. "He's like a spoiled child."

That autumn there was a violent storm. A number of trees on the estate were torn up by the roots. To the master's regret, the two ancient trees with the birds' nests were among those that were blown down. The birds beat on the manor windows with their wings, shrieking their anger.

"I suppose you're happy now, Larsen," said the master. "The storm has brought the trees down, and the birds have fled to the wood. Soon there'll be nothing left to remind us of the old days. It's very sad."

The gardener said nothing. He had long ago thought what he would do with this sunny area once the trees were gone. He meant to make it the most beautiful part of the garden.

The big trees had destroyed the old topiary hedges in their fall. In their place, he planted shrubs and trees from the countryside—the kind of plants no other gardener would think worthy of a garden. Each was planted in shade or sunshine, depending where it would thrive, and all were tended with loving care.

Junipers from the heaths of Jutland raised themselves high like Italian cypresses. The wild green holly was a delight to the eye in summer and winter. Ferns of many kinds grew like miniature palm trees. The burdock—which is despised as a weed—blossomed with flowers worthy of any bouquet. In damper soil, the common dock spread out its sculptural leaves. Mulleins like giant candlesticks, woodruff, primroses, lilies of the valley—each plant had its place. It was a joy to look at.

In front was a row of espaliered pear trees, specially imported from France, and tended so carefully that soon they were bearing as well as they would have done in their homeland.

Where the two old trees had stood was a flagpole flying the Danish flag, and a second pole twined with sweet-smelling hops. In the winter, a sheaf of oats was hung from this pole for the birds to eat at Christmastide; it was an old custom.

"The good Larsen is getting sentimental in his old age," said the master. "But he's a loyal old stick."

In the New Year, one of the illustrated papers carried a picture of the manor house, with the flagstaff and the sheaf of oats. It singled out the sheaf of oats, saying how refreshing it was to see the old traditions kept up in this way.

"Whatever Larsen does gets a fanfare," said the master. "He's a lucky man. We ought to be almost proud to have him."

But they weren't proud. They knew that they were the master and the mistress, and they could turn Larsen off with a month's notice if they chose to. They didn't, because they were decent people. There are many like them, which is just as well for the Larsens of this world.

That's the story of "The Gardener and His Master." Make of it what you will.